Cozy Up
to Trouble

a novel about a tower,
celebrity, a cat, and murder

by Colin Conway

Cozy Up to Trouble

Cover design by Zach McCain

ISBN: 979-8-9852049-1-9

Original Ink Press,
  an imprint of High Speed Creative, LLC
1521 N. Argonne Road, #C-205
Spokane Valley, WA 99212

For Noahstradamus

You can't help getting older,
but you don't have to get old.

\-   George Burns

Chapter 1

When the elevator car dinged its impending arrival, Skeeter Dursky lifted his head. He'd been staring at his scuff-free work boots and pondering the choices that led him here.

The *here* he considered wasn't the physical place where he stood holding a red toolbox in his right hand and a bucket of plumbing materials in his left. That place was the Lake Michigan Tower, a retirement community overlooking the body of water of the same name.

Skeeter rarely wasted time contemplating his existence. That sort of thing only happened while in prison, which he planned to avoid seeing again. Instead, he ruminated about being alone in his mid-thirties. He'd been by himself since leaving home as a teenager. However, it seemed the past several weeks were the most relevant for this self-assessment. Skeeter had met a girl he couldn't forget and hoped to see again someday.

He shook those thoughts away as the elevator settled noisily into place. Soon, he would board the car and begin his next task for the day—if the doors would ever open.

His gaze lifted to the floor counter above the neighboring elevator. It had been at the top—the seventeenth—but was now descending.

Saxophone-heavy jazz music filtered through

the lobby speakers. Nearby an automatic air freshener misted out a timed scent; it smelled of cinnamon and pumpkin—a reminder of the impending holiday.

Next to Skeeter, Otto Cantrell grunted. "That smell." Otto was the building's maintenance supervisor. He made a face and disgustedly wiped a finger under his nose. "It's like Thanksgiving threw up."

Part of Skeeter's new job was customer service—the worst part, it seemed. Even though he didn't feel happy, he forced a smile. Skeeter wanted to present the best image possible to whomever exited the elevator. Since today was only his third day, he was trying to make a good impression on everyone he met. The elevator still hesitated to open, which left Skeeter grinning at a closed lift.

Otto glanced sideways at him and scrunched his nose. "You call that a smile?"

"What's wrong with it?"

"You look like an ax murderer."

Skeeter's smile evaporated, which seemed to make Otto happy.

Even in heavily polished work boots, Otto was a good six inches shorter than Skeeter and more than thirty years older. It was hard to determine the man's exact age, and Otto never felt the need to reveal it.

The older man furrowed his brow. "What's up with these doors?"

As if on command, the elevator opened, and four silver-haired women appeared. Each was dressed in a pair of nicely pressed slacks and a vividly colored blouse. Their faces seemed to brighten upon recognizing Otto Cantrell.

Before arriving at the Lake Michigan Tower, Skeeter learned that being polite went a long way with regular citizens. He opened his mouth to utter a phrase of civility, but Otto stepped in front of him and spread his arms wide—a showman stealing the limelight.

"Good *morning*, ladies. You're looking lovely today—especially you, Shirley."

The four women surrounded the older man. Each said, "Good morning, Otto," in some nauseatingly sing-song fashion. After that, they beamed and tittered about the man.

Otto relished the moment.

Only Shirley Tilson noticed Skeeter, and she did so because she had to step by him to get closer to Otto. When she bumped into Skeeter's toolbox, it caught the hem of her blouse and pulled it wide. She harrumphed, quickly pulled the garment free, but didn't bother to say anything to Skeeter.

He was a large man with broad shoulders and thick arms. It was unusual for people not to pay some attention to him. Even if it was due to fear, they usually noticed him. With the long sleeves of his work shirt down, only a tattooed fireball on his right hand remained exposed. On those rare times he rolled up his sleeves, the copious amount of ink on his forearms was revealed. The tattoos often got stares—if not outright glares—from older folks. Most of the residents at the tower, however, acted as if he were invisible.

Perhaps it was his clothes. Like Otto, he wore a drab-green uniform that made him look like an overripe avocado. Skeeter's grandmother once told him that clothes make a man. These garments made him an assistant maintenance technician.

Maybe it was Skeeter's age that caused the residents to disregard him. He was probably half the age of everyone that resided in the building. But wouldn't that be an endearing quality to them? Skeeter's grandmother adored him, yet these four women seemed unimpressed.

To give the ladies more room to shower Otto with attention, Skeeter shuffled awkwardly back. His arms were tired from the weight he held. He knew better than to put either item down and risk one of the women tripping. Otto would likely lecture him for it, and Skeeter didn't want to listen to another diatribe on workplace safety. The older man loved to hear himself speak when he perceived Skeeter doing something wrong.

It frustrated him that Otto didn't offer to carry anything, but the older man insisted it was a perk of being the supervisor of maintenance. There were only two of them in the maintenance department, so a supervisor hardly seemed necessary.

Behind the women, the elevator doors closed, and the floor counter soon ticked upward.

One of the silver-haired women asked,

"What's on today's schedule, Otto?"

"Well, Skeeter and me—"

"*Who*?" they said in unison.

Otto thumbed toward the younger man, and the ladies turned expectantly toward him. It was as if they genuinely noticed Skeeter for the first time. He forced another smile.

All but Shirley Tilson recoiled at his expression of kindness. One of the ladies muttered a breathless, "Dear Lord." Shirley harrumphed a second time as she continued to rub her hip.

After Skeeter's smile faded, the ladies faced the older man.

Otto spread his hands in a what-did-I-tell-you gesture to Skeeter before continuing his story for the women. "As I was saying, Skeeter and me are on our way to fix a garbage disposal on sixteen."

"Oh," one of the women cooed as she moved closer to Otto. "My bedroom door needs attention."

Another woman touched the maintenance supervisor's forearm. "Well, my bathroom fan needs you, too. It sounds terrible, just horrible." She pursed her lips and blew an odd-sounding raspberry.

The ladies glared at their buzzing friend until she stopped.

A third woman sidled up to Otto. "The garbage chute in my hallway smells like cabbage." Her nose crinkled. "Do you know what I mean? It's so unbearable. You should come and smell it for yourself."

If the ladies were flirting, it was the worst display of the art Skeeter had ever seen. Perhaps flirting was a skill that diminished with age.

Shirley Tilson said, "And don't forget the chairs for our book club." She clapped twice as if excitedly praying. "It's going to be a big day. I can't wait."

Otto lifted his hands to quiet them. "Ladies, please. If you want to get on my schedule, you must book an appointment. You know that's how it works."

Shirley appeared ready to say something, but the other women cut her off by groaning their displeasure.

"I know, I know," the maintenance supervisor said. "There's only so much I can do. I'm just one man."

Skeeter loudly cleared his throat.

Otto eyed him. "Got a frog stuck in there?"

Shirley spoke now. "But I *am* on the schedule, Otto. I requested the dayroom weeks ago."

The maintenance supervisor smiled kindly toward her. "In that case, I'm sure we'll get it whipped into shape for you. I'll personally see to it, Shirley."

Now, the other women said happy things to Otto like, "You're so sweet. Will you put a good word in for me?" and "What would my humming refrigerator ever do without you?"

Otto looked earnestly at Shirley, but she didn't say anything. She simply smiled at him, obviously pleased that the chairs would soon be set up for the book club.

The second elevator dinged as its car settled noisily into place. While the women continued their strange flirtations with Otto, its doors opened without hesitation. A tall, silver-haired man stepped out. His shoulders were pulled back, and he stood ramrod straight. His hair had a businessman's cut and his skin a ruddy complexion. He was a model of success and confidence.

The four women quickly abandoned Otto and gravitated toward the handsome man. Their faces took on a different appearance than before, but again they jostled for position. Laughter and lilted voices now came from the women.

Flirting, it seemed, was not a diminishing art. It just needed the right target.

"Go on," Otto muttered. His gaze settled on Shirley Tilson. "Who needs you?"

Skeeter whispered, "Who's that guy?"

"Mason Freemantle." The supervisor frowned. "Thinks he's the BMOC." When Skeeter didn't register recognition, Otto added, "The big man on campus."

"Why's that?"

"Because he writes stupid books."

"Yeah?" Skeeter eyed the tall man again. "Have you read any of them?"

Otto scoffed. "He wishes."

The group of four women nudged each other as they vied for a better position with Mason.

The author seemed to enjoy the ladies' attention as much as Otto did a moment prior. Mason smiled broadly back at each of them.

The first floor's lobby opened through the second floor to create a more expansive ambiance. This allowed a group of female residents to briefly pause at a railing above and watch with envy as Shirley Tilson and her friends surrounded the author. These women soon hurried toward the elevators but kept a watchful eye on the activity below.

Skeeter said, "He's popular with the ladies."

Otto grunted.

"Especially Shirley."

"I haven't noticed." The supervisor angrily turned toward the elevator. "Aw, heck, kid. You let it close. Why'd you let it close?"

"I couldn't get around your fan club."

"They aren't my fan club." Otto glanced back toward Shirley Tilson. When Mason Freemantle said something, she laughed and touched the author's arm. "She's only nice because I fix stuff."

"You seem disappointed."

The supervisor spun around and pointed at Skeeter. "Don't go getting any ideas."

"About what?"

Otto stabbed the UP button. "Once you learn how to fix a thing or two, they'll pretend they like you, too."

"I can already fix things."

Otto mashed the UP button again. "This thing is really slow."

Skeeter said, "I know how to fix a lot of things, in fact."

The supervisor stepped back as if to survey the elevator, but Skeeter knew it was to get a better view of Shirley Tilson's flirtations with Mason Freemantle. Otto said louder than necessary, "I might have to call the elevator guy." Now, he shook his head and put his hands on his hips. "Yup. It's gonna throw the whole day off schedule. I won't have time to set up those chairs for the book club. The guest might not get to read today. Too bad."

Only Mason looked in the maintenance supervisor's direction, and the two men made eye contact. The ladies jostled more now that the author's attention was diverted.

Smugness crossed the author's face, and Otto's features tightened before he looked away.

"Bah," he grunted.

Mason said something to the ladies and led his entourage away. Shirley Tilson seemed to be the one in the brightest spirits and spoke loudly. The words 'book club' could be heard from her as the group walked into the nearby dining facility.

Otto punched one fist into an open palm. "I hate that guy."

"I can see that," Skeeter said.

The older man punched his hand again. "I mean, I really hate him. Someday, he'll get his."

Skeeter smiled. This time it felt natural. "You're just jealous because of Shirley."

The maintenance supervisor eyed the

younger man then flicked his hand dismissively. "You don't know nothing."

"I know plenty."

"I'd be surprised if that were ever true."

Chapter 2

Even though he was dressed nicely in a pair of blue slacks and a yellow sweater, Floyd Ketterling was on his hands and knees. He was trying to see what was going on underneath the kitchen sink. The balding man pushed his glasses up the bridge of his nose before asking, "Need some help?"

"Nope," Otto Cantrell said. He lay on his back with his head and upper body inside the cabinet. His legs were bent, which caused his pant legs to pull up. This revealed a pair of white tube socks peeking out above his heavily polished work boots.

Skeeter stood nearby, ready to hand tools to Otto as needed. It may be the least essential function he'd ever served, and he felt sort of foolish for it. Skeeter had rebuilt motorcycles, framed out rooms, and fixed a sink or two in his life. But Otto didn't care to know about any of those previous accomplishments. As far as the self-proclaimed maintenance supervisor was concerned, Skeeter's only ability was as a pack mule.

And the person who got Skeeter this job gave him one task—don't make waves. Therefore, as much as he disliked being an assistant and slogging tools around, he kept his thoughts to himself.

Next to Floyd, Beatrice Ketterling assumed a hunched-over position with her hands on her knees. She also tried to see under the kitchen sink. Beatrice wore slacks and a sweater that matched her husband's coloring. "Are you sure you don't need help, Otto? Floyd's pretty clever with a screwdriver."

A hand appeared and waved away Mrs. Ketterling's offer. "I'm fine."

"I know how to fix these things," Floyd said. "I did some puttering back in Oak Park. Bea always had a honey-do list ready."

Beatrice added, "Floyd helped when the repairmen came to our home, too. They were always appreciative of his expertise."

As with the ladies from the elevator, the Ketterlings mostly ignored Skeeter and concentrated on the maintenance supervisor.

Otto's hand appeared from under the sink. "Spanner."

Floyd also extended his hand toward Skeeter. Even though Mr. Ketterling didn't look at Skeeter, it was a small gesture toward the big man's existence. Therefore, Skeeter handed the adjustable wrench to Floyd. The balding man looked up with genuine surprise, and a grin spread across his face.

It was the first time since his arrival that any resident in the tower had smiled at Skeeter. He felt as if he might have made a friend.

"Spanner!" Otto angrily wriggled his fingers.

"Here you go." Using two hands, Floyd gently placed the tool in the supervisor's outstretched palm.

Otto's head immediately popped out from under the sink. He glanced at the still-smiling Floyd then glowered at Skeeter. "I asked you for the wrench."

"Floyd wanted to help."

"You are the help. You." Otto disappeared under the sink. "Not Mr. Ketterling."

Floyd shimmied closer to the opening. "I thought about doing this myself."

He smiled at his wife then turned back to Otto. "You know, seeing as it's such a minor repair and all. But I don't have any tools here. You understand."

Otto grunted in frustration. It sounded as if he smacked the garbage disposal with the wrench.

"On account of no space," Beatrice added. She leaned further over and craned her neck to see what the maintenance supervisor was doing. "It sure looks like you could use Floyd's help under there."

The supervisor's head popped back out. His face was red, but not from exertion. He faced Skeeter and pointed the wrench. With controlled calm, Otto said, "Take the Ketterlings into the other room."

"Don't you need my help?" Skeeter asked.

Floyd nodded. "Yeah, don't you need our help?"

Otto's eyes narrowed. "I was fine before you arrived, Skeeter. I'll be fine after you're gone."

The younger man straightened. "Where am I

going?"

"Don't get rid of him." Floyd motioned toward Skeeter. "I sort of like this guy."

The supervisor grimaced before disappearing back underneath the sink.

Floyd scooted a little closer to the opening and pushed his glasses back up his nose. "So, you're using a spanner wrench?"

Otto grunted.

"Did you know that 'spanner' is also slang for an incompetent person?"

"Skeeter!" Otto yelled from under the sink. "The other room!"

"Maybe we should give him some space," Skeeter suggested. He motioned the Ketterlings toward the living room.

As they moved out of the kitchen, the radio on Skeeter's hip squawked. "*Otto, this is Lorraine. I need you and the new guy to see me when you're done.*"

Otto replied, "Yeah, okay. Probably thirty minutes or so."

Another squawk from the radio. "*That'll be fine. There's been a change to today's schedule.*"

Again from the kitchen, but this time it did not come through the radio, Otto said, "Why even bother to set a schedule if you're just going to change it? Let's live like undisciplined children." It sounded as if he hit the garbage disposal. "Go where we want, do what we want, when we want." There was another clang on the disposal. "Total anarchy."

Various pieces of expensive-looking furniture

filled the living room. An oversized loveseat, recliner, and coffee table huddled in the middle of the room. A display case featuring memorabilia and tchotchkes stood alone on the nearest wall. Artwork resembling blueprints was proudly displayed. In the corner sat an older box TV.

Mr. Ketterling sat on the loveseat, and his wife settled in next to him.

Skeeter moved toward the window. One of the things he enjoyed about this new location was the views it afforded. Apartments on the north side of the building had views of Lake Michigan and Lake Shore Drive. Those on the south, like the Ketterlings, had views of Chicago. He glanced down at the parking lot; it was nearly full.

"I've done that before," Floyd said. Skeeter turned to him, and the older man motioned toward the kitchen. "Back in Oak Park, I replaced a disposal."

Beatrice patted her husband's hand. "He sure did. With another repairman, of course, but Floyd was wonderful at it."

Mr. Ketterling beamed at his wife's compliment.

Skeeter returned to where the couple was seated. "I understand. Otto doesn't want my help either."

On the coffee table were two copies of *Maine Line Murder* by Carrie Fenton. Skeeter pointed at them. "Why do you have two of the same book?"

Beatrice's face brightened. "For our club. Do you read?"

Skeeter nodded.

"What are you reading?"

"The second Travis McGee novel."

Her lips disapprovingly tightened. "*Fiction.*"

Floyd contemptuously waved his hand. "We don't waste our time on the stuff. It's cotton candy for the brain—like television."

"Only worse," Beatrice said, "because words go right into your brain."

Skeeter didn't know anything about that. Until recently, it had been a long time since he'd read a book. Oh, he would read a repair manual when needed or the occasional newspaper article, but he'd only discovered the joy of reading a book by struggling through the first McGee novel. He did that to impress Daphne Winterbourne—the girl he couldn't seem to forget. Now, he was working his way through the second. He was a slow reader, but he finished at least a few pages each day.

Floyd rolled his eyes and exhaled haughtily. "And the people who write fiction novels—insufferable bores."

"Like Mason Freemantle," Beatrice said. "He lives here, you know."

Skeeter nodded again. "I saw him this morning."

"Did you see the Masonites?" she asked.

Floyd gently touched Beatrice's arm. "It's the Freemantles, dear."

"Oh, that's right. The Freemantles. That's so

much better."

Mr. Ketterling leaned forward conspiratorially and held his hand to the side of his mouth as if he were about to share a secret in public. "That's what we call the ladies who fawn over him—especially the Tilson woman. Whenever Mason is around, she acts like a starstruck schoolgirl. Imagine that? And at her age, too."

Beatrice joined her husband in leaning forward and now held her hand in the same fashion as he did. "It's because they don't have husbands any longer." She nodded knowingly, but Skeeter didn't see what the problem was.

Mrs. Ketterling clarified it. "They're on the loose, and they treat the tower like it's a singles' bar. You're probably too young to know what those are. Horrible, nasty things." She patted her husband's arm. "That's why I have to protect him."

Floyd pushed his glasses back up his nose. "What would I do without you, dear?"

The Ketterlings kissed like two junior high school kids sharing their first romantic moment—lips puckered and bodies apart.

Picking up one of Carrie Fenton's books, Skeeter said under his breath, "I thought these were only local books."

Beatrice turned from her husband's smooshed lips. "Have you read them?"

Skeeter stiffened. It seemed a harmless utterance, but the woman had seized on it. He didn't want to lie now. He'd met Carrie several weeks ago while living in Maine, and now he was in Chicago. How likely was it to blow back on him? "I met her once," he said.

"She's a nice girl," Beatrice said. "A bit intense, though."

Floyd added, "It's probably her subject matter. All those murders and dastardly deeds. She knows her stuff, though."

"Her books really get me." Beatrice shook her hands in childlike excitement. "I'm so thrilled she's coming to see us again."

Skeeter's brow furrowed. The harmless utterance didn't feel so benign now.

Floyd scooted to the edge of the couch. "Are you okay, son? It looks like you've seen a ghost."

Skeeter had trouble swallowing. "Carrie Fenton is coming here?"

"Isn't that wonderful?" Beatrice pointed to the floor. "She'll be here today."

Floyd adjusted his glasses. "It'll be the third time she's spoken to our book club."

"What are the odds?"

Mr. Ketterling shrugged a single shoulder. "I'd say they're quite high, seeing as Shirley Tilson is her grandmother, and Thanksgiving is right around the corner."

"But the odds of her grandmother living here..." Skeeter said. He let his thought trail off.

"The world's a smaller place than you imagine," Floyd said. "We're just lucky that Shirley Tilson lives here."

Beatrice added, "But she is a Freemantle, so there's that."

"There is that." Mr. Ketterling frowned. "Still,

Carrie visited the last two times a book of hers came out."

"Who cares if she's coming because it's Thanksgiving or because one of her books is due out? We're fortunate that she comes here at all. Her visits are better than those kids selling cookies."

"I thought we liked the cookies," Floyd said.

Mrs. Ketterling squeezed her husband's hand. "They get to be a little much."

"Are we talking about the cookies or the children?"

"Yes," Beatrice said, then faced Skeeter. "Does Carrie know you're working here?"

He shook his head.

"Then you'll be able to surprise her."

"Oh, it'll be a surprise, all right."

Chapter 3

"I'm surprised you don't like country music," U.S. Marshal Gayle Goodspeed said. "Seems like it should be right up your alley."

Beauregard Smith's head rested against the passenger-side window. He grunted a noncommittal response. They were on Interstate 80 in Goodspeed's Chevy Impala.

The marshal inhaled on her cigarette before continuing. "Absentee father, messed up mother, raised by your grams, in and out of prison, and never been in love. Your whole life is heartbreak, Little Sister." She pointed at the radio. "This should be the music of your soul."

Country music never connected with Beau. He wanted the anger and angst from bands like Black Label Society, Slipknot, and Lamb of God. He even enjoyed classic rock from acts like Mötley Crüe, Black Sabbath, and Iron Maiden. If he was forced to listen to it, he could even tolerate the Beatles—not that silly nonsense about holding hands from their early years, but the later stuff like "Helter Skelter" and "Come Together."

Nothing was worse than seventies country music, though. Or as Beau thought of it—disco country. Like the song on the radio now. It was about searching for love in all the wrong places. Beau wanted to punch the singer and say that's what love was about. Grow up and add a guitar riff to it.

When the next song started, the woman behind the steering wheel reached over and turned it up. Ash dropped from the cigarette burning between her fingers. "Oh, boy, this one's a beaut. Real catchy, too."

Goodspeed didn't bother looking at Beau for feedback. He hadn't commented on her musical choices since southeastern Oregon. By then, they'd driven for almost six hours after she rescued him from a pack of Satan's Dawgs—the outlaw biker club he'd turned rat on.

Southeastern Oregon was radically different than the famously lush northwestern portion. Large swaths of the area were dry, drab land. In this section of the Pacific Northwest where tumbleweeds grew was where Beau made the mistake of saying, "This music is making me dumber."

By then, the two of them were irritable and tired from driving through the night without sleep. They were hungry, too. To be honest, it wasn't Beau's first comment about the marshal's musical taste. He had needled her for hours. At first, she took the comments in stride, but as his snide remarks continued, Goodspeed became quieter.

Eventually, the comment that the music was making him dumber proved to be the straw that broke the camel's back. Or, in this case, the marshal's tolerance.

Goodspeed slammed the brakes and yanked

the car to the side of the road. "Get out."

Beau looked around. A tumbleweed bounced by.

"I said, get out."

He faced her. "It was a joke."

"Country music isn't a joke, Little Sister."

"That depends on the listener."

In a fluid motion, Goodspeed removed the service weapon from her hip. It was such a smooth action that it surprised Beau. He hadn't expected the frail-looking woman to move with such efficiency.

"Don't make me shoot you," she said.

He figured she was bluffing. Since this was a new protector-protectee relationship, she had to reaffirm the pecking order. Instinctively, Beau understood this. The same thing happened with his previous witness inspector. That man slugged Beau early on to let him know where things stood. Oddly enough, Beau respected him because of it. That's what Goodspeed was doing now. She was too small and old to strike him, so brandishing a weapon was her way of establishing dominance.

Cops, he thought. Regardless of the badge, they were all the same.

Beau climbed out of the vehicle. Now, she would lecture him about going along to get along or some such nonsense. Again, cops were—

The car accelerated, and the passenger door slammed closed. A plume of exhaust wafted behind the Impala. The Chevy crested the rise to the east and disappeared.

He hadn't expected her to leave him on the roadside. That seemed a dangerous thing to do to teach him a lesson.

Beau crossed his arms and frowned. Okay, maybe the music wasn't *that* bad. It was only a song about sleeping single in a double bed. Perhaps he could have pretended to like it to get along. But Goodspeed was an irritating woman who insisted on calling him silly insults he didn't understand. *Little Sister?* What the heck was that? She'd been calling him that since she picked him up in Belfry, Oregon when she rescued him from some men bent on killing him.

Beauregard Smith was in the Witness Protection Program and Goodspeed was his replacement witness inspector. She was to provide him with a new identity and a place to hide. His previous inspector was laid up in a hospital somewhere, still recovering from a gunshot wound that was earned while helping Beau escape an ambush in California.

Beau was the former bookkeeper for the Satan's Dawgs, an outlaw motorcycle club based in Phoenix, Arizona. The Dawgs used coded titles for important roles within the organization. His job was to keep the book on those who crossed the club. A long line of injured and even dead men showed how efficient Beau was at clearing the books.

An FBI agent had coerced him to rat out his former associates. Had things been like they were when he first joined, he would never have flipped. But too many things had changed. The club was no longer about brotherhood; it was about money. And the leadership had begun loaning Beau's skills out to other clubs. He did what he did out of loyalty and brotherly love—not for mercenary reasons. Hurting people for financial gain wasn't something he could abide by.

Because he turned on them, the Satan's Dawgs were now after Beau. They found him in Maine. They almost caught him when he was relocated to California. And they would have killed him in Oregon if Gayle Goodspeed hadn't rescued him.

Beau looked west and saw another rise. He was in a small valley—not a good place to be stranded.

"She'll be back," he said to himself. "This is only a lesson."

Then he started counting. *One-one-thousand. Two-one-thousand.* When he reached one hundred, that seemed more than enough time to teach him a lesson. He was in the middle of nowhere without a cell phone, and his current identity was compromised.

Along with the Satan's Dawgs, the mob was also looking for him. Not just a local organized crime family either, but the entire mafia network. Years ago, someone connected with the mob had created a site on the dark web to track informants in the witness protection program. With the help of his previous inspector, Beau visited the site and found his entry on it. Now, every mafioso who had an internet connection and a password could see his picture along with artist renderings of what he might look like with different hair combinations.

Beau wasn't afraid of much, but he knew what would happen if the Satan's Dawgs caught him. The best he could hope for is that it would be quick. It definitely wouldn't be painless.

If the mob caught him, what would happen? Probably the same.

He resumed his counting again. *One-one-thousand. Two-one-thousand.* When he reached another one hundred, he reassured himself that the marshal was simply trying to show him who was boss. That's what they're supposed to do, right? Break a person down much the same way a cowboy tames an obstinate bronco.

Beau considered walking but held onto the belief that the marshal would return.

"Another hundred," he said to himself and started counting again.

While the numbers climbed slightly higher, Beau's doubt grew. Would Marshal Goodspeed actually abandon him out here? Would she do such a thing over a slight to country music? Beau didn't know her. Maybe this was how she usually acted. Perhaps those witnesses who crossed her ended up alone and exposed. That couldn't be true, could it? She wouldn't have made it very long in the marshal service if it were.

Maybe it was just him that caused her such consternation.

A group of motorcycles roared from the west. Beau flinched and quickly chided himself for the reaction. But it was a natural response.

The Dawgs had been chasing him for weeks now. He barely escaped them in Belfry, Oregon. Could they really have tracked him to this remote portion of the state? They'd already found him on opposite sides of the country. Half a state might be a cakewalk for them.

Beau spun and searched for a place to hide. There was nothing but arid land around him. Nothing provided concealment. He could run but to where? The wide-open?

His heart pounded with fear and Beauregard Smith hated that feeling. He stiffened.

No, he decided. He would not run, he would not hide, and he would not be afraid. Instead, he would stand his ground and face his fate.

Beau turned toward the oncoming bikes. He spread his feet shoulder-width apart and balled his fists. Leaning slightly forward, he prepared for the oncoming battle. Whatever man and machine hurtled his way, he would take them on—a Spartan warrior facing the oncoming horde.

The bikers appeared now—a group of ten.

Like a condemned man preparing for his death, Beau hollered, "Bring it on!"

But as the group got closer, he relaxed.

The riders were on the monstrosities known as touring bikes—motorcycles made for couples. They were citizen bikes with brand names like BMW, Honda, and Yamaha. One bike even had a small yellow flag attached to the back of its bike—it featured the University of Oregon logo.

As the motorcycles passed, the men and women riding them smiled and happily waved. One rider even flashed a peace sign, and the woman riding with him blew a kiss.

After the motorcycles faded into the distance, Beau decided to head east. He didn't know where the nearest city was but standing around wouldn't get him anywhere. And the blast of fear-inspired adrenaline bothered him.

He'd only taken a couple of steps when the Chevy Impala came back over the eastern crest. It passed him, flipped a U-turn, then pulled alongside. The window lowered.

Goodspeed leaned over. With a burning cigarette between her fingers, she motioned him back inside. "I don't have all day."

He thought about protesting but being in the marshal's car was better than being roadside. There was tough, and then there was smart.

As they drove away, Beau said, "If the Dawgs found me, they would have killed me."

"Maybe." Goodspeed shrugged. "At least you would have learned your lesson."

That was a day ago, and he hadn't commented on her music since. Now, they were in Nebraska and doing seventy-five miles per hour along Interstate 80.

Beau eyed her. "When am I getting my new alias?"

"We're picking that up in Lincoln. You'll have

some time to study it and get familiar with it."

"What's my new name?"

Goodspeed glanced at him. "Let it be a surprise."

"I hate surprises."

"You're going to love it."

"Tell me."

"No, but I'll give you this much. I named you after my favorite artist."

Beau's eyes shifted to the radio. If she were to name him after a country music star, how bad could it be? He thought about some of the names he'd heard since they'd started this drive—Hoyt Axton, Conway Twitty, Kenny Rogers, and Glen Campbell.

"I hope it's Hoyt." Beau eyed her. "That would be a cool name."

Goodspeed chuckled. "It ain't Hoyt, and if you guess it, I'll change it. Now, sit back and shut up."

She turned up the radio. The song was something about going eastbound and down.

He put his head back against the window. "We're going to Chicago. Don't the marshals only put witnesses into small towns?"

"Our job is to protect you, Beau. If you keep standing out in small-town America, let's try something different."

"Aren't you worried about the mob finding me? It's Chicago, after all."

"Where you're going, it's not going to be a problem. Nothing exciting ever happens there. Peace and quiet are the name of the game."

Beau closed his eyes. "That would be nice."

"All you got to do is keep your head down and stay out of trouble." She peered at him from the driver's seat. "Can you do that?"

"How hard could it be?"

Goodspeed grunted and turned up the music.

Chapter 4

Otto Cantrell leaned on the office chair's wooden arm and stared at Skeeter. "What do you think?"

After the maintenance supervisor finished the garbage disposal replacement in the Ketterling apartment, Skeeter returned their tools to the maintenance room located in the basement. Otto went ahead to the building manager's office and instructed Skeeter to meet him there.

He arrived a couple of minutes after the conversation started. Skeeter still didn't know quite what was going on and was trying to get up to speed.

"Well?" Otto said.

"It's a—" Skeeter searched for a better word, but not finding it, decided to repeat what the maintenance supervisor had already said. "A travesty, I guess."

"See?" Otto turned to the woman behind the desk and lifted a triumphant hand. "What did I tell you? A travesty. Our day is ruined."

Lorraine Bagley was an attractive woman in her mid-forties. She had short red hair, a turned-up nose, and freckles from cheek to cheek. She wore a green blouse and a black mini skirt. A black suit jacket hung over the back of her chair.

She contemptuously eyed Skeeter before

turning to the maintenance supervisor. "Your day is *not* ruined, and this was already on your schedule. As far as I can tell, you're making great progress today."

"We can't do it," Otto said. "Get someone else."

"There is no one else."

"Have Charlotte do it."

"This is a maintenance job, not an assistant manager's. Besides, this will take you two no more than ten minutes. In the time we've been talking, you could have set them all up."

Otto grunted. "We got more important things to do."

Lorraine leaned forward and rested an elbow on her desk. "An author's reading is important for the morale of our residents. And the book club is one of the most supported entities. Do you want to upset a third of the building?"

Lorraine turned to Skeeter again, but he looked away. He didn't want to set up for the author's reading any more than Otto, but he'd already called enough attention to himself by agreeing with the maintenance supervisor. If he could hide out during Carrie Fenton's visit, Skeeter would like to do just that. But he couldn't say that to either Lorraine or Otto.

That was because he still wasn't sure who Gayle Goodspeed's contact was within the Lake Michigan Tower.

Who helped her get him placed here? No one had come forward to say they knew about his predicament, and Gayle insisted that nobody inside the tower knew.

But Skeeter believed someone had to know. How else did he get the job without an interview? He was reluctant to ask and bring further attention to himself.

Maybe there was another answer, though.

In Maine and California, the U.S. Marshals owned the businesses that they placed him in. Perhaps the government owned the Lake Michigan Tower, too. If that were true, were all the residents in the protection program? It would be like those science fiction reruns he watched as a kid with his grandmother. The thought boggled his mind.

Lorraine pointed at Skeeter. "If you don't want to do it, Otto, give the job to the new guy. He can do it by himself."

Otto seemed offended by the suggestion. "No, he can't."

"Why not?

"He doesn't know how."

"To set chairs in a row?" She studied Skeeter now. "He looks like he can handle himself in a tough situation."

The maintenance supervisor scoffed. "He's needed on other jobs."

Lorraine rolled her eyes. "Enough, Otto."

The older man crossed his arms.

"What's this really about?" she asked.

"Nothing."

"It's not?" she scoffed. "You've set the room up plenty of other times without complaint."

From the corner of his eye, Skeeter watched

Otto. The older man had seemed willing to set up the chairs when Shirley Tilson asked. Could he really hold a grudge over her flirting with Mason Freemantle? Shirley was a resident, and Otto was an employee. He couldn't possibly believe there was an opportunity to be with a woman like her.

Lorraine now rested both of her arms on the desk and observed the maintenance supervisor. "Unless you've got a better reason, you're doing it."

Otto's gaze bounced around the room before it finally returned to the manager. "Fine, fine. We'll get it done. It's just that— Well, you know that I hate the man."

The man?

Skeeter fully faced the maintenance supervisor now. "Who are we setting up the room for?"

"Mason Freemantle," Otto said. "Who'd you think we were doing it for?"

"I thought it was for Carrie Fenton."

Lorraine leaned forward. "Shirley Tilson's granddaughter?"

"That's who Mrs. Tilson wanted it for?" Otto said. He turned his attention to Lorraine and groaned, "She's back again?"

The manager rolled her eyes. "I hope not. She's nothing but trouble."

Skeeter chuckled. "Tell me about it."

Both the manager and the maintenance supervisor eyed Skeeter. "You know her?" they asked in unison.

"Uh—" Skeeter muttered. He needed to come up with a quick story. He'd just arrived at one when Lorraine continued speaking.

"Doesn't matter. Mr. Freemantle came in this morning and reserved the dayroom for an author reading. So, it's his."

Otto said, "But Mrs. Tilson—"

"What about Shirley?"

"She reserved it for her book club."

"No, she didn't."

The maintenance supervisor appeared conflicted. "But Shirley knows the process."

Lorraine smirked. "Oh, now I see. That's what this is about. We all know you're sweet on her."

Otto looked sheepishly away.

"Fraternizing with the residents is strictly forbidden. You've had the training just like the rest of us."

He turned back. "Talking to her isn't fraternizing. Besides, she's sweet on Mason."

The manager clicked her tongue against the back of her teeth. "No, she's not."

"I think Otto's right," Skeeter said.

Lorraine's gaze snapped to the big man. "She's sweet on Mr. Freemantle?"

"No," Skeeter said. "About the book club."

"Oh."

"Maybe about Mason, too."

Lorraine's brow furrowed.

"But for sure, the book club," Skeeter said. "The Ketterlings told me that Carrie Fenton was the guest speaker today, so it seems that Shirley would have booked the room for her granddaughter."

The manager glared at him. "For a new guy, you sure are pushy."

Skeeter raised an apologetic hand. "This might be a stupid question, but can't there be two readings on the same day?"

Otto leaned over and whispered, "Are you signing us up for more work?"

"Can't we just leave the chairs set up? It would be the same amount of teardown time."

Even though he didn't want to see Carrie Fenton, Skeeter didn't understand why a second reading couldn't be held. Or why they couldn't do both at the same time, or one after the other.

Before Otto could respond, Lorraine emphatically tapped her desk.

"There will only be one reading today. Mr. Freemantle reserved the room for the entire afternoon. If Shirley Tilson wanted to schedule something, she should have done so earlier. Her granddaughter will have to wait until tomorrow." The manager put her finger on the calendar. "Well, that won't work either. It's booked solid, too."

From where he sat, Skeeter could see the calendar. There appeared to be no entries listed where Lorraine's finger pointed.

He asked, "Wasn't the book club already on our schedule for today?"

"Yeah," Otto said. "Weren't we already supposed to set up some chairs?"

"If Mason came in this morning, who

scheduled the previous meeting?" Skeeter felt proud of himself for catching the inconsistency in the manager's story.

Lorraine's face flattened. "I scheduled it."

"You?" Otto asked.

"Yes, me." The manager leaned forward and scowled at Otto. "Do you have a problem with that? The book club meets every month about this time, and I put it on the calendar—just in case."

Otto's ears reddened. "You blocked us out? Just in case? Come on, now."

Lorraine's features hardened further. "What are you implying, Otto? And tread lightly. Your annual review is coming up."

The older man flopped back into his chair. "I'm not implying anything. Never mind me. I don't know what I'm talking about."

"So," Skeeter said, "if the room was already booked, then what was the schedule change you called us about?"

Her features relaxed now. "After you set up the dayroom, Otto needs to look at elevator one. I'm getting complaints about how long it's taking to open."

"We saw," Otto muttered. "I'll check it out."

The door to the office opened then, and Mason Freemantle appeared. Skeeter turned fully in his chair to get a better view of the newcomer. Otto glanced back but quickly returned to his position facing forward.

Mason smiled broadly, and his gaze swept over the room before settling on the manager.

"Excuse me, Rainey, my dear. Didn't mean to interrupt."

Lorraine's face flushed, and a smile spread over her lips. "It's okay. Anytime, Mason." She coughed slightly and eyed the two maintenance men. "Mr. Freemantle."

"Mason, by all means." The author stepped entirely into the room now, and the door clicked behind him. His shoulders were pulled back, and his chest thrust forward as if he were about to receive a medal. Skeeter imagined many might see him as imposing. "I wanted to make sure everything was set for my reading."

She seemed to sparkle in his presence. "We're good to go." Her smile faltered as she glared at the maintenance men. "Aren't we, boys?"

Skeeter nodded once, but Otto muttered, "If we have to."

Lorraine harshly whispered, "You most certainly have to, Otto." She straightened with an embarrassed giggle. "Everything is set."

"Good. Good." Mason placed a hand on Otto's shoulder, and the maintenance supervisor stiffened. "The world needs its role players. Thank you for playing yours."

Otto attempted to shrug the man's hand off, but Mason didn't seem offended. He simply patted the shoulder. "Good ol' Otto. Dependable as an old pair of galoshes."

The maintenance supervisor's hands balled, and he gritted his teeth. Lorraine glowered at Otto.

At the bottom of the door, Skeeter noticed a

shadow move outside the office. It lingered in the hallway. Perhaps someone was coming to visit Lorraine but heard the voices inside. They hadn't knocked yet. Maybe they were waiting for a moment to see if the room would soon clear out.

"Who's the new man?" Mason asked.

The manager extended her hand. "This is Skeeter Dursky. Our new assistant maintenance man."

"Skeeter Dursky?" Mason leaned back and looked down his nose. "Good Lord, son, what part of the holler did your mother hail from?"

His file said he was from a small town in Ohio, but he wasn't about to claim that. The author seemed the type to find fault in any revelation. Skeeter didn't fear Mason, though. In his former life as an enforcer, he would have put a man like this in the hospital for cracking wise. But as the kinder, gentler now-Skeeter Dursky, he simply shrugged.

"A man of few words," Mason said. "Probably for the best. Who knows what sort of dialect would roll out?"

"What are you reading today?" Lorraine asked.

A grin burst across the author's face. "Something no one has heard before. It's my latest manuscript—*The Denver Debacle.*"

The manager leaned forward. "You're giving us a sneak peek?"

"Of course. It might be a little raw, but I'm so excited by the story I can't wait to share it."

"We can't wait." Her eyes shifted to the maintenance men. "Can we, boys?"

Skeeter and Otto murmured vague interest.

Mason Freemantle covered his heart, and his head shook with practiced affection. "As always, Rainey, you've rescued me from a pit of despair. My heart will be forever grateful."

Blossoms of cherry appeared on her cheeks, and she glanced nervously between Skeeter and Otto. "Oh, Mr. Freemantle."

"Let me grace you this evening with some wine and my time."

She nervously chuckled before saying, "I would love to."

"Fraternizing," Otto mumbled.

Lorraine frowned at the maintenance supervisor.

Mason tapped his brow then spun his hand toward her. "The time is up to you, my dear. You know where to find me." He stepped toward the door and paused.

The shadow from the hallway moved away. Perhaps they were expecting the door to open and were making way for the room's occupants to leave.

"Oh, my dear," Mason said. "Would you schedule one of the boys to come and look at my toilet?"

Otto groaned.

"The handle," Mason said and wriggled his fingers. "It jiggles a little too much for my liking. I'm worried it may fall off."

Lorraine nodded. "I'll get it scheduled. Otto

will be up right after he sets up the dayroom."

"Dependable Otto," Mason said. With a flourish, he left the office.

When the door clicked shut, Otto said, "That man needs a good swift kick in the teeth, and I'm the guy to supply the boot."

Lorraine's face flattened, and she pointed an accusatory finger at the maintenance supervisor. "You are not going to make me look bad. Set up those chairs, fix the elevator, then find out what's wrong with his toilet. Got it?

"We got it," Otto said, "but we don't like it."

"You're not paid to like it," Lorraine said. "You're paid to follow orders."

Otto stood and mimed a salute. "Aye, aye, skipper."

Skeeter followed the supervisor out of the office.

Chapter 5

Skeeter hefted one end of the table while Otto struggled with the other. They moved it from the center of the room to the furthest wall. For Skeeter, it wasn't much effort, but Otto's face purpled. The older man wheezed as they waddled with the heavy piece of furniture.

Over the dayroom's speakers, Frank Sinatra's "Fly Me to the Moon" played. He knew the members of the Rat Pack and their collected works because his grandmother listened to them. She would often put on music while she cooked in the kitchen. When Skeeter was young, he would sit at the table and talk with Ma as she worked. Occasionally, she would sing along with a song and encouraged Skeeter to do so as well. He remembered that she especially liked this one.

When they set the table in place, Otto collapsed onto it. After the second gasp of air, he said, "I hate that guy."

"I figured."

The maintenance supervisor gasped again. "He grates me." Otto now rested his head on the back of his hands.

Otto looked up. "It wouldn't be so bad if the guy wasn't such a terrible writer."

"I thought you didn't read his books."

"I don't," he grumbled. His forehead plopped

onto the back of his hands.

"Then how do you know?"

"People talk."

"What people?"

"*People*. I don't know." His voice was slightly muffled as the older man spoke directly into the table. "Besides, what do you care if I read them? It's not like you read."

"I read."

The older man's head popped back up like a jack-in-the-box. His face pinched. "You read? Like what? The back of a cereal box?"

"I'm reading a John D. MacDonald book."

"Who the heck is that?"

"A writer."

Otto frowned. "Smart aleck. Name somebody else I might know."

"Well, Agatha Christie is my favorite. I also like Sue Grafton and Janet Evanovich." Skeeter had never read those authors. He'd only heard their names when he ran a mystery bookstore in Maine.

"With the way you look, I would never have taken you to be a reader."

"My grandmother said to never judge a book by its cover."

Otto's face scrunched. "Why would she say something stupid like that? How else are you supposed to judge a book?"

"By reading it, I suppose."

"Sometimes, the cover is the best part." He waved for Skeeter to follow, and they walked to the center of the room. "Grab six of them chairs—" He pointed to several stacks lined along the wall. "—and put them in a line right here. We need five rows. Think you can do that?"

Skeeter smirked. "Thirty chairs. Got it."

"I'll be the judge, Mr. Multiplication." Otto returned to the long table, bent at the waist, and rested on it. "So, the Ketterlings told you about the Fenton woman?"

"That's right."

"While I worked, and you kibitzed."

Skeeter picked up two chairs. "You told me to."

"A goldbricker's story. So, how'd the two of you meet?"

In a previous witness protection assignment, Skeeter lived in Pleasant Valley, Maine. He lived under a far cooler alias then than the one he had now. While there, Carrie Fenton and her friend robbed a local mobster. Beau ended up involved in that crime because the mobster threatened Daphne Winterbourne. Unfortunately, that story didn't fit with the cover story Gayle Goodspeed insisted he learn for this alias. So, Skeeter told the one he was about to spill in Lorraine's office.

"I fixed her car."

Otto's eyebrow lifted. "You were a mechanic?"

"I told you I had some skills."

For the club, he'd done a variety of rebuilds on bikes to cars to tow trucks. There was also the maintenance sort of things like replacing brakes, axles, and electrical systems. Skeeter even painted a Chevy Nova with a horned barking dog—the logo of the Satan's Dawgs.

Skeeter plopped the two chairs down in the center of the room and faced Otto. With pride, he said, "If it's got an engine, I can fix it."

"Ain't that special, Gomer Pyle? If we find a car inside the tower, I'll be sure to give you a call."

Skeeter understood the Gomer reference and didn't appreciate it. As a kid, he watched reruns of *The Andy Griffith Show*. He grabbed a couple more chairs.

Otto asked, "What'd you do to the Fenton woman's car?"

"Rebuilt the carburetor."

Otto waved his hand. "Pshaw. Anyone can do that."

"Can you rebuild—"

"Stop crowing like you did something remarkable!"

Skeeter chuckled and plunked the chairs next to the others. He wasn't bragging about the carburetor. He was telling the truth. It felt good not to fabricate a story about his past. Besides, most of the guys in the club didn't know how to rebuild a carburetor. Some didn't even know what a carburetor did.

"And don't act like the Fenton woman is so special," Otto said. "I met her, too. The last time she was here hawking her books. She isn't anything great."

Skeeter collected another two chairs. "No?"

"She talked too much about Maine. Everything was Maine this and Maine that." He waggled his hands and hips whenever he said Maine.

"Isn't that the theme of her books?"

"Well, it's stupid. It can't be that nice of a place."

Skeeter thought the northeasterly state was extremely nice, especially since that was where Daphne lived. But he couldn't admit that under his current cover, so he said, "I hear it's nice."

"What do you know?" Otto walked toward the center of the room and dropped onto one of the chairs Skeeter had just placed there. "Maine sits up there all by its lonesome, acting like it's better than the rest of us. They got lobsters and lighthouses and what else? I'll tell you what else they got. Nothing. We've got lighthouses here, and we can get lobster from any grocery store. So, they're no better than us."

Otto seemed to have an irrational dislike for Maine. It wasn't a rational hostility like Skeeter had for Canada or the club's hatred for Minnesota. Those were based on reasonable things like terrible temperatures, an overly polite citizenry, and an unhealthy affinity for hockey. Skeeter thought about arguing with Otto about Maine, but what was the point? People with irrational ideas rarely see the folly in their viewpoints and arguing with them only decreases the chances they ever will.

"What was the trouble she caused the last time she was here?"

"Wasn't just the last time," he said. "It's every time. The woman stirs the pot wherever she goes. I think it's those books of hers."

"About Maine?"

"Eh." Otto waved his hand at Skeeter. "Don't be stupid. I'm talking about true crime now. She gets all the residents up in arms that someone they know is a killer or famous jewel thief, or you name it. Whenever she leaves, the book club spends days running around the tower trying to solve mysteries that don't exist. Imagine a bunch of busybodies investigating a crime that might have existed. It makes all our jobs so hard. They get me digging through the trash for things they think are clues—" he shuddered. "It takes all of us to stop them from going places that are dangerous."

"Like the roof?"

"No, like Comiskey Park." When Skeeter didn't get what Otto was saying, the maintenance man added, "Go Cubs? Ah, never mind."

A female voice could be heard in the hallway, and Otto bolted up from his chair. He ran a hand over his hair. "How do I look?"

"Like a maintenance man."

Shirley Tilson walked in with her arm hooked through a younger woman's. Carrie Fenton wore a light sweater, black jeans, and tan boots. A crimson headband held back her golden-brown hair. A slouchy bag draped over her shoulder.

"I just wanted to check how the room is coming along," Shirley said. "Then we'll get a snack and—"

"*You!*" Carrie exclaimed.

Skeeter forced a smile.

"Ax murderer," Otto whispered. "Knock it off."

The big man's face flattened.

Carrie stalked across the room, pushed aside a chair, and continued until she stood in front of Skeeter. She pulled her purse tightly to her. "What are you doing here?"

Skeeter glanced to Otto then Shirley before focusing on Carrie. "I work here."

Her eyes widened. "*Here?*"

He nodded.

"They put you here?"

Otto stepped over to Carrie. "Who are *they*?"

She blinked. "Uh."

"Is this about your carburetor, ma'am?"

"My what?"

The maintenance supervisor motioned toward Skeeter. "That thing he fixed in your car. He did a bad job, didn't he?" Otto sized up the big man. "See? That's why I'm not letting him touch anything until I show him the ropes. He just looks butterfingered." Otto wiggled the fingers on both hands. "Like a monkey with a football."

Shirley Tilson moved closer to her granddaughter, "You know this man, Honey?"

Carrie nodded. "I do. This is..." Her voice trailed off.

The big man extended his hand. "Skeeter Dursky, ma'am. Of the Ohio Durskys."

Shirley warily shook his hand.

Carrie's eyes narrowed. "*Skeeter?*"

"Named after my grandmother's favorite

country singer."

Otto leaned in and studied Skeeter. "You never told her your name when you fixed her car? That's terrible customer service. Explains a lot about you."

Shirley tapped her watch. "The room is right on schedule, Honey. Let's get you a sandwich and then—"

"Mrs. Tilson," Skeeter interrupted, "I think there's been a misunderstanding."

"What could that be?"

Expecting the maintenance supervisor to step forward and break the news to Shirley Tilson, Skeeter looked toward Otto. However, the older man glanced around as if he weren't paying attention to the conversation. He adjusted a chair that was already in perfect alignment with its neighbors. Skeeter almost expected Otto to break into a nonchalant whistle. When the supervisor's gaze finally returned to Skeeter, he opened his hands in an I-don't-know-what-to-tell-you gesture.

Skeeter frowned and faced Shirley. "The room wasn't reserved for you."

Shirley clasped her hands. "But I put in the request a while ago. Lorraine said it was mine."

"She told us it wasn't."

Shirley looked to Otto. "Is this true?"

The maintenance supervisor shrugged. "That's news to me, Shirley. I don't know anything about it."

Skeeter loudly cleared his throat to get Otto to own up to what he knew.

The maintenance supervisor slapped Skeeter's back. "Need a cough drop, kid? That frog in there is really something."

Carrie touched her grandmother's hands. "It's okay, Nana. If it doesn't happen—"

"No," Shirley said. "I requested it. This room should be ours. There are rules, and I followed them."

"I understand," Skeeter said.

"Well, I don't." Shirley's eyes were slitted.

"Me neither," Otto said. "I'm on your side." He moved to stand closer to Shirley. "We'll get to the bottom of this. I promise."

"Who got the room?" Mrs. Tilson asked. "It better not be the political action committee. If it is, I swear I'll never bake something for them ever again."

"Mason Freemantle," Skeeter said. "He reserved the room."

"Mason?" Shirley's hand touched the side of her face as a smile appeared. "Oh, well, if it's for him, then I understand. He's such a wonderful—"

"Dog!" Carrie exclaimed. "That lying, dirty dog!"

Shirley's attention snapped to her granddaughter. "Honey!"

Skeeter eyed Otto, but the older man only smiled.

"Did you tell someone the room was for me?" Carrie grabbed her grandmother's arms and looked intently into her eyes. "You did, didn't you?"

Shirley said meekly, "I might have mentioned it to Mason."

"Why would you do that?" Carrie looked toward the ceiling. "He took it because of me!"

"Now, Honey," Shirley said, "we don't know that."

"I know!"

Mrs. Tilson shook her head. "Mason isn't that type of man."

"Yes, he is, Nana! He most certainly is."

With a wide grin, Otto repeatedly pointed at Carrie. "Listen to that woman, Shirley. She knows what she's talking about. Mason Freemantle is a scoundrel."

"He did it to me again." Carrie clutched her purse tighter and turned in a circle. "He's ruining my life."

Skeeter considered intervening but thought better of it. He needed to keep a low profile. Carrie Fenton already knew his real identity and created a problem now that she knew he was here. As soon as he could, he would have to contact Gayle Goodspeed and let her know.

"Honey," Shirley said, "tell me what's going on. You're not making any sense."

Carrie angrily kneaded her purse strap. "This is the last time Mason Freemantle takes something from me."

Shirley reached for her granddaughter, but Carrie batted away her hand.

"No, Nana! This is the last time!"

"Honey, *please*. You need to calm down."

Carrie's face reddened. "Heed my words.

When I find that man, I'm going to kill him."

Otto laughed. "Let me know if you need some help."

"I'll strangle him," Carrie said. She mimed choking the man to death.

"Hitting him over the head is probably better." Otto pantomimed hitting the man with a heavy object. "A good clubbing will take less time and would be immensely more satisfying."

"Good idea!" It was Carrie's turn to point. "Got a baseball bat handy?"

"A monkey wrench would work just as good."

"You're not helping," Skeeter whispered.

The maintenance supervisor grinned wider. "It's Mason Freemantle, kid. Something bad couldn't happen to a nicer guy."

Carrie's face was now beet red. "I've had enough of that guy." She stalked away. The heavy purse bounced around her waist as she left the room.

Shirley tried to stay up with her granddaughter. "You don't mean any of that, Honey."

"Yes, I do," Carrie shouted. "Mason's days are numbered!"

Otto cast a sideways glance to Skeeter. "What did I tell you? That woman is nothing but trouble." A sly grin grew on the older man's face. "But it's happy trouble today."

Chapter 6

After finishing in the dayroom, Skeeter and Otto took a break. They walked together toward Skeeter's room. He lived in the tower's east hallway, which also housed the kitchen and the laundry room. It was the noisier of the two hallways.

As part of their compensation, both maintenance men lived on-site and received free meals. Along with the assistant manager, they were the only employees to be afforded such benefits.

Their studio apartments were on the first floor, albeit in different hallways. He had glimpsed Otto's once from the hallway while waiting for the man, and it seemed roughly the same size as his. He suspected the assistant manager's unit to be the same, although he had never seen hers.

"I'll come get you in thirty minutes," Otto said. With that, he veered into the kitchen in search of a snack. Several people of various nationalities were busy preparing that afternoon's lunch.

"Skeeter!" the kitchen crew yelled and waved.

He returned their greeting.

Angel, the head chef, came over. He was a round man with a genial face. "Want something to eat, my new friend? We can whip up a treat."

He snapped his fingers. "Just like that."

"Thank you, but I'm good."

"It is your loss." Angel patted Skeeter's shoulder. "We will see you at lunch."

Upon opening the door to his room, Skeeter was met with a low trill followed by a chirrup. An orange cat turned circles in the middle of the room.

"Travis, what did you do?"

On the floor was John D. MacDonald's *Nightmare in Pink*, the flip phone he'd left underneath his pillow, and an unopened can of cat food. The lamp was turned over on the nightstand. His pillow was scrunched and pressed against the far wall on the bed—an apparent victim of a morning brawl.

"Let me guess—the pillow looked at you funny?"

The tom trilled as he ran over to rub against Skeeter's leg. He gently pushed the cat away with his foot. "We're not those kinds of friends."

Skeeter picked up the inexpensive cell phone and opened it. Before he called a number that he'd recently committed to memory, Skeeter turned off the maintenance radio on his hip. He wasn't sure if the thing might pick up what he would say on his phone call, but there was no reason to risk it.

His previous witness inspector hadn't given him a cell phone. That man believed a phone would be a temptation for Skeeter and lead him to violate the three simple rules the marshal service required of him.

Do not contact people from your old life.
Do not visit places from your old life.
Do not develop habits from your old life.

Marshal Goodspeed thought differently. She said he could buy a burner phone at any time from any convenience store. If he were going to do something stupid, there wasn't much she could do to stop it. She might be a cantankerous old bird, but there were things Skeeter liked better about her than the previous marshal.

When the call was answered, a bright feminine voice said, "Horoscope Hook-up. Helping you find the truest love in the universe. Who may I ask is calling?"

"Skeeter Dursky. I'm a returning customer."

The U.S. Marshals created fake emergency contacts so their witnesses could safely call for help. If anyone listened in, the communication would sound natural. The last number had been for a travel agency, but Skeeter broke several protocol levels to reach them during the incident in Oregon. Therefore, the marshals abandoned that cover and created a new one.

From the other end of the line, there was some clicking on a keyboard.

Skeeter moved toward the window. His apartment looked out over the parking lot. Across the way was a manicured row of hedges that appeared to be eight feet tall. On the other side of that were Lake Shore Drive and Lake Michigan, but he only knew that because he'd seen them from the upper floors. As far as living conditions went, Skeeter had stayed in worse—

especially those with bars on the windows.

The woman returned to the phone. "Yes, Mr. Dursky. I see here— Well, you're a bit of a frequent caller, aren't you?"

"A few times. It couldn't be helped."

The operator laughed politely. "That's okay. Love and happiness are hard to find."

It was a truth Skeeter couldn't argue with.

"What are you looking for today?" the woman asked.

Skeeter felt foolish saying the line Goodspeed insisted he memorize, but he did so anyway. A shadow moved near the door to his apartment just as he spoke.

"I'm a Libra, and I'm looking for a Capricorn."

"Oh, dear," the woman said. "I'm sorry, but that's not a good match."

In the hallway, the shadow remained for a moment, then it disappeared. It could have been someone walking by. Or might it have been someone coming to visit? Otto, perhaps? But it hadn't even been five minutes since the two men spoke, and he said he'd be by in thirty.

Shadows outside doors weren't uncommon in the tower. In fact, it had happened earlier outside Lorraine's office.

The operator continued. "Wouldn't you prefer a Leo or perhaps a Gemini?"

"No, I'd really like a Capricorn—preferably an irritable one who chain smokes."

"That's oddly specific," the operator murmured. More clicking on the other side of the line now. "And it isn't something most would want, but I've found one for you. She's nearby and able to meet today."

"Imagine my luck."

"It's not luck," the operator exclaimed. "It's fate! I'm reading your daily horoscope now. Wow, what a day you are about to have. It says to embrace new relationships, for they should be friendly, warm, and prosperous. Isn't that great? I'm a Pisces and my day is supposed to be filled with abrupt—"

Skeeter hung up.

After retrieving the other items that Travis knocked to the floor, Skeeter reclined on his bed and read some of his book. One of the things he enjoyed about Travis McGee was how the man thought about things. Skeeter wanted to be a more profound thinker.

Did that come as part of being a better man?

***

A knock on the door woke him. The McGee novel rested on his chest. How long had he been out? It couldn't have been more than a few minutes since Otto was supposed to collect him for their next job in thirty minutes. He tossed the paperback aside and stood. He felt groggy from the nap.

Upon opening the door, Charlotte Olsen stood there with her hands on her hips. She was the assistant manager and wore a name tag announcing as much. She was a cute woman who stood roughly five and a half feet tall. She wore a brown pant suit and a tan blouse. An eyebrow lifted playfully as a smile creased her lips.

"Taking a break, I see."

"Just a couple minutes." Skeeter blinked away the lingering effects of the nap. "I had to make a call."

"How are you settling in?"

"Better than I could hope."

Behind him, the cat trilled, and Charlotte's face brightened.

"You've got a cat!" She stepped by without invitation. The tom approached the assistant manager, and she bent to pet him. "He's wonderful."

"You like them?" he asked.

"I adore them." She looked up to Skeeter with a bright smile. "You didn't have him when you moved in. I would have remembered."

On his first evening at the tower, an unidentified man in a suit had approached him in the parking lot. Skeeter was outside enjoying a quiet moment to himself. The Satan's Dawgs were no longer on his heels, and he felt like he could finally relax. He walked to the shrubs in hopes of seeing through them—he couldn't.

For a moment, the green wall of shrubs felt like a prison, and he considered escaping. All he had to do was turn toward the parking lot entrance and run.

But if he did so, then not only would his former club and the mafia be after him, but so would the federal government. They were the biggest gang of all, and there was no need to anger them.

"Skeeter Dursky?" the approaching man had asked. Before Skeeter could answer, the suited man set two items at his feet. The first was a large paper sack. The second was a cardboard box with holes in its sides. When the man straightened, he said, "Courtesy of the U.S. government. He's your problem now."

Skeeter tried to protest, but the man sprinted toward a running vehicle. The unmarked car raced from the parking lot.

"Where'd you get him?" Charlotte asked.

"I found him."

"What a find." She continued petting the tom. "He's really something."

"He's something all right."

Charlotte checked the cat's collar for a tag, but there wasn't one. "Maybe his human is looking for him."

"I doubt that."

The cat initially belonged to the owner of the bookstore in Maine. Skeeter left it behind when he fled that state, but his former witness inspector ensured the troublesome tom found its way to California. By the time he bolted the Golden State, Skeeter had grown slightly fond of the cat. Part of that fondness was the expectation he would never see it again.

"Are you going to keep him?" Charlotte asked.

"Probably." A side of Skeeter was happy to have a friend, but he also considered that a weakness. Was that a hangover from his old life? Would a better man be worried about how a cat made him look? He deflected the self-doubt by saying, "He's sort of a menace since he's always knocking over things."

Charlotte eyed the two empty dishes that sat on the floor near the sink. "He's probably hungry and thirsty. You'd throw a tantrum, too."

In the paper sack that the government man left were all the items a new cat owner needed. It now sat next to an opened bag of kibbles and the empty bowls. Charlotte stood and refilled the food dish. As she filled the bowl, she muttered something wistful like, "A man with a cat."

He wasn't sure she had indeed said that, so he asked, "What did you say?"

She glanced back. "Two scoops a day. That's all a beautiful boy like this would need."

He was pretty sure that wasn't what she said, but he let it go.

Charlotte returned her attention to the tom. "What's his name?"

"You can pick."

It was tradition. The cat's original owner allowed visitors to the bookstore to name the tom whatever they wanted. She reasoned that the individual's naming of the cat reflected who they were. The only caveat to the rule was that the name had to be a protagonist from a mystery novel.

When Skeeter and the cat ended up in a California record store, he modified the naming rule to musicians. Now they were in a seventeen-story high-rise overlooking Lake Michigan. If he was going to alter the naming tradition, what should he change it to?

Names of famous Chicagoans? He didn't know any except maybe the sports teams, and Cub the cat sounded sort of weird.

Names of the Great Lakes? The only one he knew was Michigan, and that's because the tower sat on it.

He was at a loss for a new naming rule, but would it even matter? With Carrie Fenton in the building, it was likely Gayle Goodspeed would relocate him. This cover was already blown.

After setting down the food dish, Charlotte's eyes widened. "You're really going to let me name him?"

"Yes, but you have to—"

"Oh, man!" She straightened. "That's sweet of you, Skeeter. You're the best."

"Now, listen—"

"I've always wanted to name an orange cat Blue." Charlotte bent at the waist and ran her hand along the tom's back and up its tail. "You're the best boy, Blue. Do you like your new name?"

Travis didn't seem to mind as his nose was buried in the food dish.

Charlotte turned expectantly to Skeeter. "What do you think?"

He shrugged. If she wanted to name the cat after a color, what did it matter to him? "It's a fine name."

"You think so?" She smiled broadly and stepped closer to Skeeter. "Blue the orange cat sounds like a children's story? Do you like kids?"

"As long as they're someone else's."

Her smile faded, and she suddenly seemed disappointed. She glanced longingly back at the tom. "At least, you have a cat. That's something."

"Was there a reason you stopped by?"

Charlotte's gaze returned to the big man. "Right. Why did I come here? Oh, yeah. Where's Otto?"

"I don't know."

"You haven't heard Lorraine ordering you and me to find him?"

He shook his head.

Charlotte's gaze dropped to his radio. "Is that off?" She lowered her voice. "You can get in trouble for that. It's supposed to be on during business hours. Lorraine's a stickler for things like that."

Skeeter reached down and turned it back on. "How long's it been off?"

"Since my call." He picked up his phone and flipped it open. The call to Horoscope Hook-up was made almost an hour ago. He snapped the phone shut. Why hadn't Otto come to get him?

"Why'd you turn it off?"

"I was afraid of interference with my phone."

Charlotte smirked, but her eyes were playful. "There wouldn't be any interference. What were you really doing? You were taking a nap, weren't you?"

"No."

"When you opened the door, it looked like you had been."

He shook his head. "I was on a call. Really."

She playfully smacked his arm. "Relax. I'm not going to get you in trouble." Her hand lingered a moment on his bicep. "Wow. You must work out."

He did while in the motorcycle club and while incarcerated, but it had been a few weeks since he'd been inside a gym.

"You know," Charlotte said. "Employees can use the tower's fitness facility. Maybe we can be workout buddies." She flexed her arms. "Maybe you can show me a thing or two."

"Is that what you came here for?"

"To be workout buddies? No." She blinked. "Unless you said yes." Now, she giggled nervously. "But you didn't. Maybe we can talk about that later. Right. No, I came looking for Otto."

"Why? What's going on?"

The smile faded from her face. "Mason Freemantle was just found dead."

"He's dead?"

She nodded. "As a doornail, which is a funny expression when you think about it. What the heck is a doornail?"

"What happened?" he asked.

"I don't know, but someone says it was murder. Lorraine's up there on seventeen with the cops. She loves being the center of attention.

She's a Gemini, you know, and they love that sort of thing." She moved a little closer. "Since nobody famous has ever died here before, I'm sure Lorraine will draft a press release to get on the news."

There was something in the way Charlotte acted. It was too relaxed—almost nonchalant about the murder of a resident. Also, why did she bring up the astrological sign?

As if she heard his thoughts, Charlotte said, "I'm not too worried about the whole thing."

"You're not?"

"Nuh-uh. I'm an Aquarius," she leaned forward, "in case you didn't know."

"I didn't."

"Most people don't. And that sort of stuff—what's going on up on seventeen— doesn't impress us. We're a laid-back lot—us children of the water-bearer. What sign are you, by the way?"

"I don't know."

"Really?" She flashed a coy look. "I bet you're a Libra. You look like a Libra. Do you know what they say about Libras and Aquariuses?"

He didn't, and he didn't want to know.

"Or is it Aquarii?

"You're not concerned about Mason Freemantle's murder?"

Charlotte sighed, and her gaze drifted to the cat. "Why should I be concerned? I didn't do anything."

"I didn't say you did."

Her eyes returned to the big man. "Well, don't

go suggesting it either. This place is a gossip factory."

"Why does Lorraine want Otto?"

The assistant manager shrugged. "No idea. She just started calling for us to find him. And when you weren't answering, I got worried, so I came to check on you."

"You found me."

"Lucky for you, you have an alibi." She pointed to the cat.

"What do I need an alibi for?"

"I thought that's what the cops did—ask everyone for their alibi when someone gets murdered."

"Do you have one?"

She rolled her eyes. "Of course, I do. I was with the Ketterlings. Checking in to see if they were satisfied with the work that you and Otto did for them. They were, by the way. Mr. Ketterling seemed especially fond of you."

Skeeter shrugged. "He likes to help."

"So, about that workout—let me know if you want to go sometime."

"Okay."

"It's more fun to work out with a friend. I'm just saying." She studied him the way a shopper examines a steak in the butcher's case. "I should go." But she didn't make a move toward the door. Instead, she stood directly in front of him. "Is there anything you want to ask me?"

"No."

"You can. Anything at all."

Skeeter shook his head. "I'm good."

Charlotte inhaled deeply and pointed to the tom. "You're going to make a lot of friends with Blue. The residents love people with cats. I know I do."

And with that, she was out the door. It clicked shut behind her.

The tom rubbed against Skeeter's leg. "Sorry, Travis. It looks like you're Blue now."

His radio squawked. *"Charlotte, have you found Otto yet? Send him up to seventeen immediately. And where the heck is Skeeter?"*

Chapter 7

Skeeter stepped into the hallway and pulled his door shut. He didn't bother locking his door. It felt weird not to do such a thing, but leaving an apartment unlocked seemed to be the norm in the building. Otto explained it to him on his first day, and Skeeter's initial thought was a burglar would have a field day in the tower.

From down the hall, it sounded as if there was a lot of commotion.

To the right, an outside door led to the parking lot. Through the door's window, he could see a man standing there with his back to the building. A tingling sensation shot through him. Perhaps it was his old survival instinct kicking in, but Skeeter didn't ignore it. He'd survived too many scrapes in his life to disregard that feeling.

It wasn't necessary to walk softly in the hallway, but Skeeter did so, nonetheless. Habits in a situation like this were kept for a reason; they allowed him to live another day.

Up close now, he peered through the glass and his suspicion was confirmed. The man outside was a police officer. Stationing men to guard the building's exits was not a good omen.

Skeeter turned and headed toward the commotion at the opposite end of the hall. As he passed the kitchen, he glanced in and found it eerily silent. Even though he'd only been there for a few days, it seemed weird to see it so still at this time of day. Lunch was about to be served. Food sat out on the counters as if the people preparing it were forced to walk away from their duties mid-prep.

In the lobby, a large crowd of silver-haired folks assembled, along with the kitchen staff. They stood in two separate groups. Even in a moment of stress, there existed a division of haves and have-nots.

A lone uniformed officer did his best to quiet the onlookers. He held his hands high in the air and hollered above the cacophony of voices. "Quiet! All of you! Just shut it!"

The assembled mass calmed. Skeeter believed it was more from the disrespectful way the request was presented rather than its lawfulness.

"I'm Officer Baggiano," he said loudly, "of the Chicago Police Department, and here's what we're gonna do."

The officer didn't make for a striking appearance. He was in his late forties with a heavy paunch and a jowly face. His wrinkled uniform was untucked on the left side, and his duty belt was loose. It gave him the appearance of an aging, sloppy gunfighter.

On the second floor, several residents paused at the railing to listen to the cop below. Baggiano pointed up at them. "You! Yeah, you. Come down here."

With some resignation, the residents turned

toward the elevators.

"Now, all of you are going to talk with me—"

The crowd groaned.

"—and after we get done, you stand over there—"

"Where?" someone hollered.

"There," Baggiano pointed to an open area of the lobby. "You're gonna stand right there, so I know I've talked with you. Got it?"

An older man with a walker raised his hand. "Then can we go back to our rooms?"

"No," the cop said. "Now, as I was saying—"

Once again, the older man raised his hand. "What about lunch?"

The cop rolled his eyes. "It'll have to wait, pops. We're investigating a crime here, but since you're such an eager beaver, why don't you step over here and let's have ourselves a little conversation."

The older man appeared uncomfortable, perhaps scared, for being singled out. The room seemed to quiet further.

Baggiano snapped his fingers. "Let's go, old-timer. Pick up the pace. It's not like you people got all the time in the world."

At the back of the assembled crowd, two women stood near Skeeter. One was tall and wore a purple sweater. Her friend was much shorter and wore a yellow pullover.

"All this over that woman," the shorter woman said. "I can't see nothing, can you?"

"I can see fine. She must have been jealous."

"What gave you that clue, Edna? When she

yelled at him or when she slapped him?" The shorter woman shifted her position as she tried to look through the crowd.

"I never thought she would kill him, though." Edna stepped back so her friend could slip in front of her. "When he got on the elevator, I thought it was over."

The smaller woman looked up at her friend. "You thought it was over?"

"I did, Muriel. I really did."

"You heard what she said. What were her exact words?"

Edna shrugged. "'This isn't over.'"

"Right." Muriel turned back toward the crowd. "She said it with a lot more conviction than that, but that's what she said."

"Then she jumped on the elevator with him."

"So, it wasn't over, was it?" Muriel glanced at Skeeter.

He was about to smile, but she looked back toward the crowd. Again, he felt almost invisible to the residents. It was an odd sensation. While it might be exactly what the witness protection program should be about, Skeeter Dursky had to admit he didn't enjoy it. For his whole life, people seemed to notice him.

When he was younger, it was due to his long hair and rock & roll t-shirts. Later as he got bigger, it was due to his size. When he joined the Satan's Dawgs and developed a renegade appearance, citizens gave him a wide berth wherever he went. Now, in this retirement community, the elderly residents treated him as if he almost didn't exist. It bothered him, and he blamed the uniform.

"I bet Shirley Tilson is heartbroken," Edna said.

"For sure."

The mention of Shirley Tilson snapped Skeeter from his self-pity.

Edna said, "She's the biggest Mason Freemantle fan I know."

Muriel cast a sideways glance. "You think she's heartbroken over him? What about her granddaughter?"

"Oh, right." Edna chuckled. "But still, Mason was a pretty good writer."

"I know. A real tragedy." Muriel stood on her tiptoes and craned her neck for a better view.

Skeeter glanced around. Was Carrie Fenton involved in Mason Freemantle's murder? She *had* threatened to kill him in the dayroom. Could she have carried through with that intention?

On the far wall hung a large, round clock with a black and white face. The hands showed it was nearly eleven.

"What do they have to interview us for?" Edna asked. "We didn't see anything."

Muriel returned to her normal height. "This is what the cops do when someone's been murdered. Haven't you watched the shows?"

"I have, but they already know she did it, so can't they hurry it along?"

"They have to be thorough."

Edna shrugged. "I guess. Have you ever read

her stuff?"

"Shirley's granddaughter's?" Muriel's face pinched. "Why would I read it? She writes about Maine. Why? Have you read it?"

"I haven't. What's wrong with it?"

"Lobsters and lighthouses." Muriel shuffled anxiously. "I can't see from back here."

Now, Edna chuckled. "Right. Lobsters and lighthouses. Who wants to read about that?"

"Probably the same people who want to read about vampires and werewolves." Muriel shifted to her right.

"How do you think she got into his apartment?" Edna asked. "Do you think he let her in?"

Muriel's head whipped back to her friend. "She killed Mason in his apartment? How do you know she did that? Did I miss something?"

Edna pointed at the elevator. "That's what I figured. Why else would a cop and a detective—They're the ones in the suits, right?"

"Hey, Big Bird, I'm down here at ground level. I didn't see anyone in a suit."

"A lady in a suit went into the second elevator."

"Maybe she was with the property management company. Ever think of that?"

"She had a gun." Edna mimed a pistol with her thumb and forefinger. "Pew pew."

"Interesting." Muriel faced into the rear of the crowd. "So, Shirley's granddaughter killed Mason Freemantle in his room."

"That's what I'm thinking. So, how do you

think she got in there?"

Muriel looked up at her friend with a face contorted with disbelief. "Hello? She's a writer, and those folks are a diabolical lot." She tapped her temple. "Real nasties. They're always thinking about how to get away with murder. I bet most writers probably have a hundred ways to kill someone without getting caught. And you know they keep a list of all those ideas just so they never forget."

Edna's face tightened, and she had trouble swallowing. "I thought what they wrote was only make-believe."

"That's why they're diabolical. They *want* you to think that." Muriel's eyes brightened, and she tapped her temple again. "And you just know those devious types keep their how-to-kill lists out in the open so their friends and family can see it. They're not showing off to the world. What they're doing is building an alibi. They get to say stuff like, 'That's for a story I'm working on,' then laugh all the way to the bank. It's the murderer's long game."

"It is?"

Muriel nodded. "How many writers do you know have been arrested for murder?"

"None."

"There you go. That's statistically impossible. Don't you think?"

"I never thought about it."

Muriel shook her head. "See? They've lulled all of us to sleep, yet every day they're practicing murder. Visualizing it until it's perfect." She shuddered. "I bet most writers have a body buried in their backyard. Put that in your pipe."

"Jimmy Hoffa," Edna said. "He probably knew a writer."

"What do you want to bet? Let's get closer. I want to get interrogated." Muriel pushed into the crowd. Edna shrugged and followed her friend.

As the crowd parted for the two women, Officer Baggiano finished interviewing the first witness. He turned in time to see Skeeter standing alone at the back of the group. "Hey, you. Come over here."

Just to make sure, Skeeter glanced to his left and right to be sure the cop didn't want someone else.

"Yeah, you. The big avocado." Irritation laced Baggiano's voice. "Who else am I looking at? Mayor Daly?"

When he was with the Satan's Dawgs, Skeeter's former self would have stood his ground and made the cop come to him. Willful disobedience was his default setting when confronted by law enforcement. Until his run-in with the FBI, cooperating with the cops was never an option. However, since landing in witness protection, he'd developed a slight change of heart.

Skeeter headed toward the cop, albeit slowly.

"Come on, come on," Baggiano groused. "These geezers don't have time for your lollygagging."

He walked slower.

The cop shifted his weight and rested his elbow on the gun attached to his right hip. His left hand fiddled with a cell phone attached to the duty belt. Baggiano's gaze dropped to Skeeter's uniform. His mouth smacked as he chewed a piece of gum. "You work here?"

"So they tell me."

The officer's gaze dropped to the tattoo on Skeeter's hand. "What's that?"

"A tattoo."

"No, tough guy." More gum chewing and lip smacking. "What's it mean?"

"That I make bad decisions."

Baggiano's elbow slid back off the gun until his hand rested on the handle. He stopped chewing, and his lips pressed tightly together. Skeeter wasn't intimidated, though. Maybe if they were on a back road somewhere, but the officer wasn't likely to try something in a retirement community. "You don't like cops much."

"Don't take it personally."

"Hard not to." Baggiano's mouth returned to working on the gum, and he waggled two fingers. "Lemme see some ID."

Skeeter handed his license to the officer.

The cop whistled after reading it. "Skeeter Davis Dursky. Your parents must have hated you."

"They named me after a famous country singer."

The cop shrugged. "You got me. I've never heard of him."

"Her."

"You were named after a woman?"

"It was either that or Sue."

Baggiano paused in his gum chewing, and his eyes went up as he thought. When he latched onto something, the smacking resumed. "No wonder you got such an attitude. What do you do around here?"

"Assistant maintenance man."

Baggiano copied Skeeter's license information into a notebook. "What'd you see?"

"Nothing."

"How'd you see nothing?"

Skeeter shrugged. "It's a big building. What was I supposed to have seen?"

"A confrontation here in the lobby."

"Between?"

"Mason Freemantle and a woman." The officer consulted his notebook as he moved his gum around with his tongue. "Carrie Fenton. Those names mean anything to you?"

"Mr. Freemantle lives in the building. Never heard of the other person."

Even though his previous life was filled with criminal activity he'd like to forget, there were many valuable things Skeeter learned. One of them was to only talk to the cops when necessary—until then, keep quiet. Right now, sharing what Carrie said in the dayroom about Mason Freemantle wasn't crucial to his freedom.

Baggiano shifted his stance. "So, you've never met this Fenton broad?"

"Does she live in the building? Maybe I've seen her."

The officer fiddled with Skeeter's driver's license. "Do you know of anyone who would want to hurt Mr. Freemantle?"

Carrie's threat to kill the author rang in Skeeter's ears. "No, but I didn't even know the man existed until today."

The officer quit fingering the ID card. "How could you not know Mason Freemantle? He's one of the biggest authors ever. Twenty or so of his books have been made into movies. He's a legend."

"I've only worked here for three days."

The officer stepped back and reconsidered the bigger man. "Three days?"

"That's right."

"And Mason Freemantle ends up dead. That's a heck of a way to start your employment."

"It's not ideal."

The cop's eyes narrowed. "Might also be a coincidence—you start here and him winding up dead. You ever been in trouble with the law?"

"Do parking tickets count?"

Baggiano's gaze dropped to the license.

Skeeter asked, "If Mason Freemantle is such a legend, why isn't he in a mansion with all sorts of personal help?"

"Don't you follow the news?"

"Not really."

"The story goes that Freemantle's manager embezzled millions from him about a decade ago. Before that, Freemantle had to spend a bunch of money defending himself against plagiarism. He won that case because he was a living legend."

"You already said that."

"And I'll say it again if I want. The guy was my favorite, and there was no way he would steal another man's idea. I mean, c'mon." Baggiano absently waved his hand. "Besides, this place ain't cheap. You should know that. A lot of wealthy people live here."

"I'm just saying."

The cop flicked Skeeter's license with his middle finger. "I know what you're saying, Skeeter Davis Dursky, and I don't like it. It seems as if you aren't a fan of Mason Freemantle."

"I didn't even know the man."

"You said you met him."

"That's different than knowing him."

Baggiano smirked. "Yeah, yeah. Where were you when he was murdered?"

"How do I know when he was murdered?"

"Let's say thirty minutes ago. Where were you then?"

"In my apartment."

Baggiano's eyes darted about the lobby. "You got a room *here*?"

"I do."

The edge of the cop's mouth quivered. "Can anybody confirm you were there?"

"My cat, but he's not much of a talker."

The cop flicked the driver's license again. "Some attitude you got."

"So, this Carrie Fenton. Did she kill Mason?"

"We suspect her."

"So, you're not sure."

Baggiano smiled. "You're sure a smart one, aren't ya? Don't worry, Einstein, we're sure the lady did it. We just have to say that we suspect her to keep the brass happy. You know, they always want to have a little wiggle room, just in case."

"In case you're wrong."

The cop's face flattened. "For the press." He shoved the driver's license back to Skeeter. "You best watch yourself."

"Am I free to go?"

"No. Stand over there and stay out of trouble."

Chapter 8

As Officer Baggiano moved to interview the kitchen staff, Skeeter stepped into a group of residents that included Edna and Muriel. The crowd seemed disappointed that Baggiano had moved toward the employees of the building and not them. The elderly residents expressed uniform excitement about their chance to be interrogated. That was the word they all used—*interrogated.*

In his previous life, Skeeter had learned the hard way that there was a difference between interviews and interrogations. An interview was better. Interrogations occurred when the cops were putting the screws to a person. Unless the cops found Mason Freemantle's killer, no one was getting that treatment today. Compared to an interrogation, Baggiano was overly polite with the residents and staff—almost gentle.

Skeeter glanced around. There was a cop outside guarding the exit doors of the lobby. He imagined another guarding the hallway where Otto's room was, too. The building was locked down. No one was getting in or out that the cops didn't want. That meant Gayle Goodspeed couldn't get to him now without badging her way in and blowing his cover.

If Carrie Fenton were to be arrested, then maybe his troubles were about to be over. He didn't hope for Carrie to be detained, though.

Fate was cruel in the previous three small towns he visited and had quickly ruined his assumed identity. Perhaps things could work out this time and he could remain here for a while. Working as an assistant maintenance man wasn't the most exciting job in the world, yet Skeeter liked it better than the alternative— relocating once more.

Officer Baggiano told him to stay in the lobby, but Skeeter wanted to do something else. He could feel that old sense of rebellion brewing in his gut. Even going back to his room so he could read his book was better than standing around. He liked knowing what Travis was up to— McGee, not the tom.

A stooped-over man with wispy hair approached. He wore a button-up shirt, blue jeans, and white tennis shoes. In his right hand was a cane with four legs. On the bottom of each leg were four cut-open tennis balls. "Are you the one that Charlotte's been talking up?"

"Excuse me?"

"She's over there." He pointed toward the west hall. "She's going on about some new fella with a blue cat."

Several people turned his way. Edna whispered to Muriel, "Did you hear that? He's got a blue cat."

Muriel shushed her and leaned in to hear the older man.

He lifted his cane slightly. "Is it true? You've got a blue cat?"

Skeeter smiled. "He's not blue. He's—"

"Bah." The older man interrupted. "She's fibbing again."

Edna and Muriel groaned with disappointment. This rippled through the crowd around them.

"His name is Blue," Skeeter said. "Like the color."

Then he glanced at the dispirited folks in the nearby crowd. It seemed weird to want them to understand. For a moment, he had something they thought was special—a blue cat—but that vanished when he clarified the misunderstanding. Now, the residents studied him with looks that bordered on contempt. He forced a smile and said, "You can see him if you want."

Muriel and Edna looked at each other then rolled their eyes.

"Mister," Muriel said to Skeeter, "that's the oldest line in the book."

"Yeah," Edna added. "We're not falling for it again."

Muriel thumbed toward the older man with the cane. "Clancy has used that tired old come-on for years."

"Never mind that nonsense," the older man said and shooed the ladies away. "Go back to your knitting circle."

Muriel stuck her tongue out, and Edna thumbed her nose before moving toward their friends.

"You've got a way with the ladies," Skeeter

said.

"And you're a wiseacre. Where's Otto?"

"I don't know. Is there something you need help with?"

Clancy pointed upward. "There's a wonky whatchamacallit in my room. Otto knows how to fix it. He's done it before."

"What's broken? Maybe I can fix it."

"The whatchamacallit." The older man swirled his cane about. "Weren't you paying attention? And it ain't broken. It's on the blink. Always comes back when Otto uses the doohickey." Now, Clancy wriggled his free hand.

"Doesn't sound like Otto fixed it."

"You don't fix what ain't broke. It's only on the fritz. Why is it so hard to communicate with you? First, your cat ain't blue, and now you don't know where Otto is. What good are you?"

The radio on Skeeter's hip squawked. "*Charlotte?*" Lorraine called. "*Charlotte, have you found Otto yet? Have you checked the maintenance room?*"

Skeeter lowered the radio's volume. "No one can seem to find Otto."

Clancy's eyes narrowed. "Oh, so now it's not your responsibility? You're one of them millenniums like my granddaughter—that's what this is. My son can't talk to her any better than me."

Muriel and Edna moved closer again. Their friends followed along.

Skeeter had never considered himself a millennial. He'd been labeled many things in his life—misfit, Dawg, convict, felon, and rat—but millennial seemed to be the one group he hadn't been associated with yet.

"Now, just a minute," Skeeter said, but Clancy ignored his protest.

"That girl is always going on about how adulting is so hard."

The nearby group murmured its disapproval of the word 'adulting.'

Clancy continued. "And then she's got the gall to humble brag whenever she makes her own breakfast." He air-quoted humble brag.

The assembled residents snickered at the phrase.

The older man frowned. "It's not like your generation invented smearing avocado over toast, but she's gotta take a picture of it every time she makes it. To share her big discovery with the world. Like she's Edison or something."

Muriel said, "Or Picasso."

"Or Betty Crocker," Edna added.

The nearby crowd murmured their support of Edna's mention of Betty Crocker. Even Muriel seemed to approve, and the taller woman smiled broadly.

Skeeter wanted to interrupt Clancy's tirade to say he'd never heard of adulting, humble-bragging, or avocado-smeared toast, but the older man lifted his cane a few inches then slammed it to the ground.

"She's a lacto-vegetarian hot yoga instructor. Dadgummit, boy, what is it with your generation? You're making up your own dadburn language!"

Skeeter cocked his head. "So, do you want my help fixing your thingamajig or not?"

"No!" The older man's face pinched. "There's nothing wrong with my thingamajig. Weren't you paying attention? It's the whatchamacallit. Make yourself useful and find Otto." He turned and angrily shuffled off.

Muriel and Edna shook their heads. Several of the residents seemed to take an unhealthy interest in him now. This wasn't the kind of notice he wanted from them.

Skeeter motioned toward the departing Clancy. "Can you believe that guy?"

"Him?" Muriel asked. "It's you we're not sure about."

Edna nodded. "Yeah, it's you."

Skeeter touched his chest. "What did I do?"

Muriel pointed at him. "First, you invited us to your room with promises to see your cat. You probably don't even have a cat."

"Masher," Edna said.

"I have a cat."

"Sure, you do." Muriel shook her head. "Then you insulted Clancy."

"Brute," Edna added.

"I didn't insult Clancy," Skeeter said. "I offered to help him. Besides, I didn't even think you liked the guy."

Muriel clucked. "We like him fine. Better than you. We had no idea how much Otto had to put up with."

"The man's a saint," Edna said.

"A living saint," Muriel agreed. "Let's go."

The two women turned and rejoined their friends. Several of them continued to watch Skeeter with open hostility. Now, they all seemed to notice him.

***

Skeeter slowly worked his way toward the opposite edge of the lobby—the side which led to the west hallway where Otto's room was.

He thought he might be able to sneak away with some others, but the residents of the Lake Michigan Tower weren't the type to openly disobey the orders of the police. They waited patiently for Officer Baggiano to get to them. Their strict adherence to following orders was why the police could post only a single officer in the lobby.

Even though the residents were obedient, they were growing less patient about it. Their cacophonous excitement about being interrogated had turned into muted dissatisfaction that the process wasn't moving along quicker. There were complaints about various subjects, but the most heard refrain seemed to be about a single topic.

"When are we gonna get lunch?" one resident complained. "Why aren't those cooks back in the kitchen?"

"Why'd the cops have to close the galley?" another chimed in. "It's not like Mason was murdered in there."

"Even if he was," yet another added, "it's not like he was killed inside the refrigerator. How hard would it be for one of those cooks to reach over a dead body and pull out a sandwich?"

A tall, thin man dressed in a fashionable sweatsuit dramatically touched his forehead with the back of his hand. He was careful not to muss his perfectly combed hair while doing so. "Do I look pale?" he asked. "I feel pale. I think my blood sugar is dropping. I think I'm going to pass out."

Next to him, three women also in sweatsuits eyed him with disdain. Their outfits did not fit them as nicely.

The tall man continued. "If we don't do lunch soon, those cops are going to be investigating two deaths."

Collectively, the women eyed the man like hyenas stalking a wounded gazelle.

"Because," the tall man said, "I'm going to starve to death. Hello?"

The group of three groaned, "We know."

"Don't worry," one of the women said. "We'll kill you long before you starve to death."

The tall man touched his forehead again. "I'm serious. Am I pale? I need to eat regularly because of my high metabolism."

Even more people groaned now. It sounded as if an opposing team had just scored a touchdown.

"Keep it down over there," Officer Baggiano hollered. "We're trying to conduct an interview."

The tall man waved at those chiding him.

"When I pass out from hypoglycemia, you'll rue this moment."

"I'm already ruing it," one resident muttered.

Skeeter continued shuffling toward the opposite side of the lobby. As he went, a couple of residents asked where Otto was. When he offered to fix whatever problem they had, the response was much the same as Clancy's: "We'll wait for Otto."

One woman with big silver hair, large earrings, and a heavy necklace did stop him. She glanced around before whispering, "How can I get a snack?"

"I don't know."

She eyed him. "You know how. I can see it. You're the type who knows things."

"Ask the kitchen crew." Skeeter pointed to the group of cooks who stood together. They were answering Officer Baggiano's questions.

The woman frowned. "I don't speak their language."

Angel, the head chef, noticed Skeeter and the woman watching him. He lifted his chin in acknowledgment. Skeeter waved back.

"Do you speak their language?" the woman asked.

"I do."

"I would never have guessed. You don't look bilingual." She glanced around again. "Find out where they're keeping the snacks, and there's a fiver in it for you."

"I have to find Otto now, but when I get back, I'll work on those snacks."

Her eyes narrowed. "You could do it now."

"That's right. I could."

Skeeter moved in the opposite direction of the kitchen. Behind him, the woman openly grumbled. When he made it to the west hallway, he simply turned and walked away. No one told him to stop. No one yelled for him to come back. No one seemed to care that he was gone.

At the end of the hallway was a door to the outside. Through the glass, he could see the back of another cop.

He lightly knocked on Otto's door. Across the hall was Charlotte's room. He wondered if she might be there now, so he didn't want to knock too loudly and call attention to himself. Her forwardness wasn't something he wanted to encourage.

There was no answer from Otto. Wondering if the maintenance supervisor kept his unit unlocked like the residents did, Skeeter tried the knob. The door opened, and he stepped inside.

Otto's unit was the same size as Skeeter's, but it had the feel of long-term tenancy. Framed photographs were on the wall. Most of them appeared to be of Otto and residents of the building. Some had inscriptions written in the corner. *Merry Christmas and Happy Hanukkah* were a couple he noticed.

The maintenance supervisor kept a clean room. His bed was made, and several pairs of polished shoes were placed in a row underneath. No dishes were in the sink.

On a bookshelf were a variety of novels. He'd seen some of them when he owned the store in Maine. When Skeeter noticed a series of books, he knelt to examine them closer.

The bottom row contained seven hardback novels from Mason Freemantle. The covers of each book appeared to be heavily worn. He pulled out the first, The Portland Squeeze. Upon closer inspection, the cover seemed to have a coffee stain on it. When he opened it, he noticed that many pages were wrinkled and had folded corners. At the front of the novel, he found a lined-through inscription.

~~To Abagail—Best Wishes!—Mason~~

Who was Abagail? Was she Otto's wife? His girlfriend? A resident?

Underneath someone else had written in blue ink,

So stupid. Same as the others.

The handwriting was clean and precise, almost feminine. He hadn't yet seen Otto's penmanship, but if this was how the man wrote, Skeeter would be very impressed.

He grabbed the next book, *The Rochester Crash,* and examined it. This book also had a stain on it, but it appeared to be food grease. Otto was a messy eater while he read. Skeeter opened the book and, just like the previous novel, found a lined through inscription.

To Hayward—Best Wishes!—Mason

Skeeter looked through the next five books. Each of them had a city in the title, and each of them had some sort of stain on the cover. Inside there was the same inscription—Best Wishes!—made out to different people. All of them were lined out.

If Otto hated the man so much, why did he have these books that were given to others?

On a whim, he flipped through the book he still held. Throughout the novel, passages were highlighted, lined out, or circled. Derogatory comments were made in the white space. At the end of one book, was a single comment—*Terrible.*

Skeeter went through the books again and checked the contents of each. Throughout were more highlights, lines, and circles. The end of every novel was met with a single word. *Dreadful. Appalling. Awful.* And so on.

He put them back. Out of curiosity, he checked the books from other authors. None of them had inscriptions, and none were marked up the way the Mason Freemantle novels were. Skeeter put the books back as they were and left the room as quickly and quietly as possible.

Closing the door, he glanced down the hallway; the cop was still outside guarding the exit. At the opposite end, the restless crowd seemed to be growing louder.

Where could Otto be?

When Skeeter had gone to his room, the maintenance supervisor had headed toward the kitchen for a bite. Otto was then supposed to collect Skeeter in thirty minutes. An hour passed before Charlotte showed up at his room. Maybe Otto left the building, but he hadn't expressed a need to leave. If he hadn't left the building, where could a maintenance man go so no one would bother him?

Skeeter had an idea. If Charlotte hadn't checked it out yet, maybe the older man would be there.

He edged two doors to the left where a stairwell led to the basement. Skeeter made sure no one was watching before stepping through.

Chapter 9

Skeeter quickly descended the stairwell. For fire safety and ease of access, another stairwell also adjoined the east hallway where his apartment was located. When Skeeter made it to the cement floor below, he called out, "Otto?"

There was a constant hum in the basement from the various running systems.

The building's boiler system was down there. Skeeter didn't know how it worked, but it provided heat for the tower. One elevator shaft came to the basement, but the mechanical systems for both cars were on the roof. The chiller, which provided cool air, was also located outside on the top of the building. Due to the season, it was currently off.

Skeeter moved through the basement and its makeshift rooms. As he went, he called out variations of "Hey, Otto," but no answer came.

There was a multitude of workbenches and shelves laden with parts and tools. Otto seemed to revel in this place whenever the two of them were down here. The older man even had a paint-spattered boom box so he could listen to an oldies rock and roll station. Whenever Otto was in the basement, the music was on, but the radio was silent now. Would the man have it on when there were cops upstairs investigating a murder? Perhaps, but unlikely. Otto wasn't the type to goof off.

Skeeter returned to the central portion of the basement. He'd noticed a box of granola bars on the upper level of a workbench. All the talk upstairs of lunch and snacks had made him hungry. With the kitchen closed, who knew when the next opportunity to eat would be. He reached for the box.

"Beau?"

His hand hovered over the granola bars. Had he heard a faint woman's voice over the droning of various systems? Or was his mind playing tricks on him? He turned but didn't see anyone.

"Come out where I can see you."

Carrie Fenton stepped from behind a shelf lined with old paint cans and through a rack of drab-green uniforms. One of the garments fell to the floor as she passed through.

"I thought that was your voice." She brushed cobwebs off her shoulders. "I couldn't see too well from back there."

He pointed at her. "You have some on your head, too."

She calmly ran her fingers through her hair. When she finished, she looked at him. "This probably looks bad."

"You look fine."

"I meant hiding in the basement."

Skeeter shrugged. "You don't have to explain. I understand."

"Of anyone, you probably do, but I didn't kill Mason."

"Then what are you hiding for?"

She threw her arms into the air. "Oh, I don't know, maybe because I freaked out! Haven't you ever freaked out?"

He motioned for her to lower her voice.

"Of course not," she said sharply. "Not Beau Smith. In the face of danger and calamity, he doesn't freak out."

His motioning became more pronounced. "Relax, Carrie. Calm down. Take a deep breath. And it's Skeeter now."

"Right." She closed her eyes and inhaled sharply. She held the air for a second then let it out through barely parted lips.

"Are you better now?" he asked.

Her eyes popped open. "Seriously? No, I am not better. I'm still in the same situation."

Once again, Skeeter motioned for her to soften her voice. "Calm down."

Carrie nodded once, then looked briefly away. When she returned her gaze to him, she asked, "What's going on up there?" She pointed toward the ceiling. "Have the cops arrived yet?"

"It's like a law enforcement convention up there. They've got the whole building locked down."

"Oh, man. I'm screwed." With both hands, Carrie held her head. "I'm really screwed."

"The only way that it could get worse is if the purple hat coalition shows up."

"The purple hat a-what-a-what?"

Skeeter dismissively waved. "Never mind. Tell me what happened."

Carrie walked over to a stepstool and sat on

it. Her position didn't appear to be comfortable. "After you told my grandmother that Mason reserved the room, I sort of lost it."

"That's putting it mildly. You said you were going to kill him."

Her shoulders slumped. "Then I made it worse when I confronted him in the lobby. We argued, and I slapped him. Actually, before I slapped him, I think I said something like—"

"'This isn't over.'"

Carrie nodded. "Right. 'This isn't over.' That's what I said, wasn't it? How'd you know? Oh, crud. There were witnesses, weren't there?"

"A few."

She hit her forehead with the palm of her hand. "What an idiot. Stupid. So stupid."

"What happened then?"

"I stepped in it."

"By following him onto the elevator."

She nodded. "The witnesses again? This keeps getting better. Well, Mason hit the button for the seventeenth floor, but I wasn't going to let that dog get away that easily. I pressed a slew of buttons to make sure we had to stop a bunch of times in-between."

"Nice."

"I thought so, but during one of those stops, he shoved me out."

Skeeter thought about how slow the elevator doors were. "You could have jumped back on."

"I dropped my purse."

"Who would steal from you in the tower? You could have come back and collected it later."

Carrie appeared sheepish. "Some of the contents spilled out."

"So? You're in the middle of an argument with Mason Freemantle, a very heated one, it sounds like, and he pushed you out."

"To be correct, he angrily shoved me out. Get it right."

"Then you dropped your purse, but instead of hopping back into the elevator to finish the argument, you take your time to pick up your lip gloss."

"It wasn't lip gloss." Carrie raised an eyebrow. "Just what kind of girl do you think I am?"

Skeeter shrugged. The girls that hung around the club always wore lip gloss. He didn't know it was a bad thing. "Okay, so you picked up your lipstick. Whatever."

"I wouldn't stop to pick up any cosmetics. For real, Beau—"

"Skeeter."

"What kind of woman do you think I am?"

With her long-sleeved sweater, Carrie Fenton looked like a mild-mannered non-fiction writer. However, Skeeter remembered that her left arm was covered in tattoos. He'd seen them while they were in Maine. And while she might not look like the type for trouble, she had robbed a local mobster who operated a money-laundering business in Pleasant Valley.

The mob was after him for helping Carrie and her friend get away with that crime. He got involved so he could save Daphne Winterbourne—the woman that he couldn't forget. The mob had no idea that Carrie and her friend stole the money. They only knew that Skeeter was involved in the mobster's death— they probably blamed him for the stolen money, too.

"I don't know what kind of woman you are," Skeeter said. "If you didn't stop for your make-up, then what did you stop for?"

Carrie looked away.

"If you don't want to tell me, I don't care. I'm not the one hiding in the basement. I'll go up to my room and chill out. The cops can handle this, and you can deal with them. It'll make my life easier."

He almost expected her to make some comment about knowing his real identity when her gaze returned to him. Instead, she said, "It was the money."

"What money?"

Frustrated, she lifted her hands in the air. "*The* money. What other money could I be talking about?" Her arms fell to her sides. "My portion of it, anyway. Or what was left of it."

He thought about her in the dayroom and how heavy her purse seemed. The bag swung about her waist as she walked. When she stood in front of him, she clutched it tightly to her waist. Skeeter looked at her now with incredulity. "You brought the money *here*?"

"What else was I going to do with it? I couldn't put it in a bank."

"You could have buried it in your backyard."

"I haven't been home since the robbery. I was

afraid to go there."

"Why?"

"Because I'm afraid they might know."

"The mob or the cops?"

"Yes."

Skeeter smirked. "The mob doesn't know about you, and I don't think the cops do either."

"I'm still afraid."

"A lock box then. You could have gone to a train station or an airport and put it in one there. Then you could have picked it up at any time."

Carrie's face pinched. "I'm not doing that. I want the money close by."

"Then secure it in a hotel safe. They've got those, you know? Anywhere else would have been better than that goofy-looking purse."

She stood and pointed at Skeeter. "Hey! I'll have you know that's a Bergdorf Goodman. It cost me three thousand."

"For a leather grocery bag?"

"That grocery bag is worth more than—"

Skeeter's gaze drifted about the area. "Where's the purse?"

Carrie's face reddened, and she looked away again.

He stepped by her and poked his head through the rack of uniforms so he could see behind the shelf. Nothing was back there. When he pulled his head out, he faced Carrie. "You don't have it."

"No kidding, Sherlock."

"So, when Freemantle pushed you off the

elevator, you dropped the purse."

"I already told you that."

Skeeter ignored her. He was replaying the scene for himself. "Some of the money spilled out of that overpriced Bergdorf Goodman."

Carrie huffed.

"You stopped to pick it up, but by the time you did, he was already on his way to the seventeenth floor."

She cocked a hip. "There are no flies on you, Detective Smith. You've got the whole thing figured out."

"Except what happened next."

Her eyes narrowed, and her lips twisted. It appeared as if she were stewing. Skeeter wasn't in a hurry, so he let Carrie seethe.

Eventually, she calmed. "Fine. Whatever. I wouldn't let it go, all right? I should have, but I couldn't."

"What did you do after you picked the money up?"

"I caught the next elevator and went up to the seventeenth."

"How long did that take?"

"For the next elevator?" Carrie's head bounced as she thought. "I don't know. A minute at most."

"You must have been pretty steamed by the time it arrived."

"Steamed? I was royally—"

The boiler hissed.

Skeeter asked, "How'd you know which apartment was his? Had you been there before?"

Her eyes bulged. "No, I'd never been there before. How many times do I have to ask what kind of woman do you think I am?"

The big man shrugged.

"Right. You have no idea. Listen, I wasn't thinking clearly. But if I had to, I would have banged on every door and made a real jerk of myself. Luckily, I didn't have to." Her face flattened. "Wait. That wasn't lucky. I take that back. Because when I got to his floor, I saw an apartment with an opened door. I looked in and saw Mason on the ground."

"He was already down? You said it only took a minute for the other elevator to arrive. Someone killed him in that short window of time? This couldn't have been a crime of opportunity. It had to have been one someone thought about."

Carrie shrugged. "I guess."

"Trust me. I know these things. What happened next?"

"I went inside."

"Why?"

She turned her palms upward. "Do you really have to ask that? I might have wanted to kill the man, but I didn't want him dead."

For the former bookkeeper of the Satan's Dawgs, it was the most incongruous statement ever made. If Skeeter's former version of himself wanted to kill a man, he most certainly wanted him dead. Even though he was trying to be a kinder and gentler person, Skeeter admitted he still felt the same way.

Carrie continued. "I knelt and was shaking him when she walked in."

"Who?"

"The manager—Lorraine what's-her-name?"

"Bagley. Lorraine Bagley."

"That's right. She walked in and yelled, 'You killed him. You killed Mason Freemantle!' She made a real production of it."

Skeeter motioned for her to keep quiet.

"Who's gonna hear me over all this noise?"

"You never know. What happened next?"

"I freaked out—plain and simple. As I ran by her, Lorraine tried to stop me. She grabbed my purse, and it slipped off my shoulder. Other residents were already in the hallway by then. She pointed at me and yelled, 'Call the police. That woman killed Mason Freemantle!' So, I hit the stairs and ran all the way down until I ended up here in the basement."

"Why didn't you go to your grandmother's?"

"That's the first place the cops would look."

Skeeter rubbed his face. "And you can't call the police because they have your bag of money."

"That's right."

"How much was in there?"

"About a hundred thousand."

"How did you fly to Chicago with that much cash?"

"Fly? I drove. As I told you, I've been on the run since we stole it."

"If your car is in the parking lot, why didn't you run there?"

She tilted her head and stared at him. "What?"

"My purse."

"Yeah, so?"

"Lorraine had it."

Skeeter said, "Leave the money. Get in your car and go to Canada."

"Maybe you're not very good at this detective thing. Where do women keep their wallets and car keys?"

Skeeter suddenly felt stupid.

"So, I only had one option."

"Run and hide."

"That's right."

Skeeter studied Carrie. "I never got the chance to ask you this in Pleasant Valley. Why *did* you steal the money? You don't seem to be the felonious type."

Carrie's head bounced like a bobblehead doll. "I write about this stuff all day long. Cops and robbers. Killers and victims. I guess I just wanted to know what committing a crime felt like."

"And what did you think?"

Remorse washed over her face. "Hand to God. If I could do it all over again, I wouldn't. I hate this feeling. The guilt. Always looking over my shoulder like someone's chasing me."

"But you got away clean."

"Because of you." Carrie plopped onto the little stool again. "I've spent the last weeks worried about someone taking the money. It's made me feel like Gollum and his ring."

"Who?"

"You know. The weird little monster that constantly says, 'My precious' in *The Hobbit* and *The Lord of the Rings*."

Skeeter shrugged. He had no idea what she was talking about.

She sighed. "Right. You were only pretending to be a bookstore owner."

"So, where's your partner in crime?"

"Probably on some island somewhere with her Italian boyfriend. She has a lot less fear and regret than I do. I guess I'm better at writing about a life of crime than living one. I've been a wreck ever since we took the money. I'd give anything to go back to my nice, boring life."

Something about Carrie's story still bothered Skeeter. It took him a moment to figure it out. Why did Carrie Fenton hate Mason Freemantle so much? He was about to ask when the elevator car settled noisily into the shaft.

"Someone's coming," Skeeter whispered. "Hide."

Carrie knocked another uniform from the rack as she moved through them on her way to hide behind the shelf filled with paint cans. Skeeter hurried over and picked up the two hangers from the floor. A pair of drab-green pants slipped from one of the hangers.

When the elevator doors opened, a police officer appeared. He immediately noticed Skeeter. "Hey, you!"

"Me?"

"Yeah, you. Who else?"

Skeeter hung the two uniforms on the rack. He hadn't rehung the pair of pants and simply let them remain on the floor.

The cop stepped from the elevator. "Are you Otto?"

"No, I'm Skeeter."

The cop was a younger man with fast, twitchy movements. He might even have been fresh out of the academy. His uniform was impeccable, and his name tag read Metcalf. He glanced around. "Anyone else with you?"

"Just me."

The cop eyed him. "What are you doing down here?"

"The kitchen is closed, so I came looking for a snack."

Metcalf's face brightened. "Find any?"

Skeeter pointed to the box of granola bars.

"Mind if I have one?"

He shrugged. "Help yourself."

The officer stepped over and peered into the box. "Chocolate covered." Metcalf pulled out two packages and slipped one into each pocket. Then he tossed the empty container into the nearby trash can. Skeeter's shoulders slumped. He should have kept his mouth shut.

"What's your job around here, Skeeter?"

"Assistant maintenance man."

Metcalf pulled a granola bar from his pocket and ripped it open. "So you know this Otto guy? Where is he? The detective wants him."

"What do they want him for?"

The cop bit into the snack bar. Through a

mouthful of food, he said, "Does my badge say detective? I do what she tells me."

"I don't know where he's at."

Metcalf eyed him. "I guess you'll have to do." He pressed the elevator's call button. "Let's go."

"If you didn't find Otto," Skeeter asked, "who set the elevator to come down here? Otto told me only the maintenance team could do that."

"How would I know?" Metcalf took another bite of the granola bar. "I'm only here for the overtime."

Chapter 10

By the time the elevator doors opened, Officer Metcalf was opening the second granola bar. "These things are great. I mean *really* great."

"They look it," Skeeter said.

Under the elevator buttons was an opened panel—it should have been closed. It contained a phone to reach emergency personnel and a keyed switch to allow the elevator to enter the basement. A yellow tag dangled from an inserted key. Skeeter had wrongly thought only the maintenance men were able to engage that switch. Someone else had the same ability. Lorraine or Charlotte seemed the obvious choices.

Officer Metcalf stepped out of the elevator and pointed down the hallway. "It's over here."

A few apartments away, sunlight beamed through an open door.

As the cop walked down the hall, he studied the half-eaten granola bar. "They taste all chocolaty, but there's an oat-y goodness inside. Know what I mean?"

"No," Skeeter said. "I don't."

"The next time I go to the store, I'm gonna have to get some of these."

The two men stopped outside the apartment, but Skeeter could see Mason Freemantle's body on the floor from where he stood. It lay face down with one arm extended above his head. He couldn't be sure without getting closer, but it appeared as if the back of Mason's head was matted with blood.

Near the body was Carrie Fenton's slouchy purse.

"Detective," Metcalf called. "Yo, Detective!"

A woman with olive skin and long dark hair stepped into view. She wore a black blazer, a purple blouse, and gray pants. In her left hand were a notepad and pen. "Is this the maintenance supervisor?"

"It's his assistant."

Her face pinched a second before her chin dropped to her chest. Then the detective stepped around the fallen man and approached the opened door. "What did I ask for, Metcalf?"

"Ma'am?"

"Did I ask for an *assistant* maintenance man?"

"No, but I thought—"

The detective pointed at the officer's hand. "What's that?"

"Oh, man, it's this chocolaty granola thing. It's so good. I'd give you one, but—"

"This is a crime scene."

With the hand holding the granola bar, Metcalf pointed into Mason Freemantle's apartment. "I thought the crime scene was in there."

The detective waved along the hallway. "The killer didn't magically appear in the apartment."

The officer looked down at the snack bar he

held. Several pieces of granola lay on the floor near his boot.

"See the problem?" the detective asked. "Why don't you put that in your pocket and go stand near the elevator."

"Yes, ma'am," Metcalf said and wandered off. He muttered to himself as he went.

When the two of them were alone, the woman extended her hand. "Detective Kajal Reddy. And you are?"

"Skeeter Dursky." He accepted her hand. Usually, he would attempt to hide the tattoo on the back of his hand by turning the palm upward, but he hadn't done anything wrong.

The detective turned his hand so she could study the inky ball of fire. "Skeeter Dursky. That seems to be a name worth remembering." She glanced up at him. "What's this tattoo mean?"

"It means I'm never going to be elected president."

She dropped his hand and moved slightly to the side. Now, Skeeter had a clear view into the apartment and of the dead man. Through the unit's windows, he could see Lake Michigan outside.

Reddy asked, "Where's Otto Cantrell?"

Skeeter shrugged. "I don't know. I've heard Lorraine asking Charlotte to find him. She can't raise him either. What do you need him for?"

Instead of answering his question, the detective consulted her notebook. "You're new around here, right?"

"Three days."

"And where are you from?"

"Ohio." It was part of his background story. Skeeter didn't like her questioning tone and hoped to stop her from going down that rabbit hole. "Am I a suspect?"

"Everyone's a suspect. Where in Ohio?"

"Findlay." He motioned toward the dead man. "I didn't even know Mason."

"But you know it's Mason Freemantle. Where in Ohio is Findlay?"

"Midwest, near Van Wert. How could I not know him? He's famous."

"You read?"

"Not his stuff."

She made a note.

"You wrote that down?"

Reddy eyed him. "I write everything down. You seem to be handling this well."

"Handling what?"

The detective pointed into the apartment. "There's a dead man over there. Most citizens balk at that sort of thing, but not Skeeter Dursky from Findlay, Ohio. To you, it's another day on the job."

"I'm trying not to think about it."

"Uh-huh. What did you do before this?"

"I was a mechanic." That wasn't in his file, but he said that in case she learned about his connection to Carrie Fenton.

Reddy made another note. While her attention was diverted, Skeeter studied the purse that lay next to Mason Freemantle. Something thin and black protruded from it. It looked familiar, and Skeeter instinctively touched his radio antenna. He was sure there was a similar unit in the purse.

The volume on his radio was still turned down, but he pressed the transmit button. From Mason Freemantle's apartment, the unit inside the purse squawked.

The detective glanced back at the fallen Mason Freemantle.

Just to make sure, Skeeter pressed the button again, and it screeched once more.

Reddy turned back to him. "Did you witness a threat today?"

Skeeter's hand fell from his radio. He wasn't about to mention what he heard Carrie say. He rolled his lip down and shook his head. "No."

"You didn't hear Otto Cantrell threaten Mason Freemantle?"

His eyebrows rose. "What? No. I never heard him threaten anyone."

Denial was the natural response to any question from authority, but she was right. Otto had threatened Mason Freemantle—several times, in fact. Skeeter hadn't taken any of them seriously. He mentally flipped through the threats he'd heard, and there was only one that Detective Reddy could know about—the threat Otto made in Lorraine Bagley's office. The others were made when Otto and Skeeter were alone.

The detective confirmed it when she said, "The manager reported Otto Cantrell threatened Mr. Freemantle. She reported you witnessed this threat."

Instead of lying, Skeeter said, "I thought you suspected a woman."

Detective Reddy seemed genuinely surprised. "Why would you think that?"

Skeeter pointed toward the slouchy purse. "I don't think that belongs to Mason Freemantle or Otto. And you wouldn't be so careless to put yours down in the middle of a crime scene—not after the lecture you just gave Metcalf."

The detective glanced down the hallway. Officer Metcalf stood at the elevator. It appeared as if he were still talking to himself.

"You're pretty observant for a maintenance man."

"Assistant," Skeeter said. He moved toward the open door and leaned against the jamb. He eyed the purse, then glanced at Detective Reddy. "How's the purse fit in?"

Detective Reddy leaned against the other side of the jamb. "What are you after, Mr. Dursky?"

"It's not Mason's."

Reddy smiled. "Tell me something I don't know. Do that, and maybe I'll share something with you."

Skeeter pretended to study the purse. "That bag is a Bergdorf Goodman."

The detective straightened. "How in the world—"

"It retails for about three thousand."

Her face flattened. "Now, that's something I didn't know. How did you?"

"I knew a girl who liked purses."

Reddy's gaze ran his length. "I bet you know

a lot of girls."

Skeeter did. At one time, he lived a hedonistic life with the Satan's Dawgs, but now he wanted to live differently. That was for many reasons, but it was spurred chiefly due to the woman back in Maine. It was quiet for a moment until Skeeter realized the detective was still observing him.

He needed to say something. "It's an expensive purse to be left at a homicide. What was in it?"

The detective returned to her place along the opposite jamb. "Besides Otto Cantrell's radio?"

Skeeter feigned his surprise. "How do you know it's his? Did Lorraine tell you that?"

Reddy shrugged.

"How do you think it got there?" he asked.

"That's what we'd like to know, but now no one can locate Mr. Cantrell."

"Who's the purse belong to?"

Detective Reddy seemed to consider his question before answering. "It belongs to a Carrie Fenton. A witness described her as leaning over Mr. Freemantle's body. Have you ever heard of her?"

Skeeter shook his head. He knew the witness Reddy mentioned was Lorraine Bagley.

The detective said, "Her grandmother lives in the building."

"And you figure, what? That this Carrie Fenton woman comes to visit her grandmother for Thanksgiving and ends up killing Mason Freemantle instead?"

"Stranger things have happened."

Still leaning against the door jamb, Skeeter crossed his arms. "How did this woman get Otto's radio?"

"My theory is they're working together."

"Accomplices?"

She nodded once.

"For what end?"

Suspicion flooded the detective's eyes. "You're pretty inquisitive for an assistance maintenance man."

"You just said I was observant."

"Okay, inquisitive *and* observant."

Skeeter needed another reason for her to keep talking, and he quickly fell back on an old ruse. "Maybe I'm neither. Maybe I'm just making time."

"Time?"

He smiled.

"Oh," she said. "I see." Detective Kajal Reddy smiled back.

Skeeter flirted a lot in his previous life. He wasn't inclined to do such a thing now that Daphne Winterbourne was on his mind, but he needed information. If showing a little interest in the detective could get him that, Skeeter would smile a little more.

The detective put her pen on her notepad. "Mr. Dursky, do you think that batting your eyes and grinning like a fool will make me weak in the knees?"

Skeeter's smile faded. It worked with the girls who hung around the club. Maybe his own flirting skills had diminished since his time as a bookkeeper.

Reddy pointed her notepad at him. "There's no chance that I'm going to go all goo-goo for you and start giving away what we know."

"You've got me all wrong. That's not it."

"It's not? Then what kind of time are you trying to make with me?"

He needed a different story, so he said the first that came to mind. It seemed something that Travis McGee might say. "I want to help."

"Help?"

"Yeah. Help. Even though I'm new here, I'm supposed to take care of this place. If something happens to one of the residents, it happens to them all."

"Since we can't make time, you're going to try out for the pope?"

He ignored her jab. "We need to wrap this up quickly—"

"We?"

"So the cops will leave our building, and the residents can return to their normal lives."

Detective Reddy pushed her lips from side to side. "I think you're shining me on."

With a finger, Skeeter drew an X over his heart. "Hope to die."

"All right. This is against my better judgment, but since you're a helper and all, I'll give you the benefit of the doubt." She jerked her head toward Mason Freemantle's apartment. "Around the corner, you can't see it from here, but there's an open safe. Everything has been cleared out."

"Mason Freemantle was burglarized?"

"Forcibly robbed. Further inside the apartment, we found a monkey wrench with blood on it." She mimed a chopping action.

Skeeter thought about Otto's suggestion to Carrie about clubbing Mason Freemantle.

"Are you missing one?" the detective asked.

"I don't have a monkey wrench."

She smirked. "I meant the maintenance office or room or wherever you types store your tools."

"It's my third day. I barely know where the parking lot is."

Detective Reddy pointed into the apartment. "What do you want to bet that tool has Otto Cantrell's fingerprints on it?"

"If it's from our maintenance department, then it's a high probability."

She snapped her fingers. "That's what he'll claim when we find him. That someone stole it, but he's not fooling me. The way I figure it, Carrie Fenton and Otto Cantrell were in the middle of robbing the safe when Mr. Freemantle entered and surprised them. He tried to leave—you notice how the body was positioned, didn't you?"

Now that she mentioned it, Skeeter did. Mason Freemantle's head was closest to them. It made sense that the man was returning to his front door.

"So, Carrie Fenton or Otto Cantrell clubbed Mason with that heavy wrench and then tossed it back into the apartment. I'm guessing Otto. A wrench seems a tool that a maintenance man would have at his disposal." Detective Reddy glanced at his waist. "I'm noticing you don't carry any tools."

Skeeter ran his hands along his belt. "They ruin the line of my uniform, but why would Otto leave the murder weapon behind? Especially if it was a tool that he was responsible for. Doesn't make sense."

Reddy shrugged. "Maybe he tossed it to establish a flimsy alibi. Just like you're thinking, it doesn't make sense and that's what they'd fall back on. The argument is that he couldn't have left it behind because it would implicate him. And if that wasn't the reason, well, people do irrational things after killing another human being."

Skeeter knew the latter statement was not true—at least, not for him while he was with the Dawgs. He always became more careful after the act. It was as if his senses became hyper-vigilant to make sure he didn't make any costly mistakes that could put him behind bars for life or worse.

"So," he said, "besides Otto's radio, what else was in the purse?"

Reddy raised an eyebrow. "I thought you forgot."

He hadn't. He knew there should be—

"Forty thousand dollars," she said confidently.

Skeeter tried to hold his surprise, but the detective caught it.

"I know, right?" Detective Reddy pointed at the purse. "I figure that's what Carrie Fenton and Otto Cantrell were after. They forced Mason Freemantle to open his safe—"

"By threatening him with a monkey wrench?"

"It's a heavy object. I'd be intimidated by it. But Mr. Freemantle made a break for the front door when they were distracted. Unfortunately, he never made it before—" she mimed the overhead clubbing action again "—one of the two whacked him on the head. Again, I'm guessing it was Otto, and he left Carrie holding the bag—both literally and figuratively."

Skeeter knew there was more to that story. Carrie had said there was a hundred thousand in the purse. That meant Lorraine probably stole sixty thousand dollars after Carrie fled the scene. The building's manager was also conveniently in the hallway of the seventeenth floor when Carrie discovered Mason's body. Was it too much of a stretch to believe that she could have killed the man?

No, he decided, it wasn't.

Before the cops arrived, Lorraine had taken some of the money. Then when interviewed, the manager provided Otto's name to the police as another possible suspect.

Is that when she put Otto's radio in the purse? If so, how did she get it from the maintenance supervisor? Did she have that much forethought in killing Mason?

But Lorraine seemed to like the famous author. What changed in such a short time that would lead her to club him to death?

Skeeter couldn't reveal to Detective Reddy any of his thoughts on Carrie Fenton's innocence. Doing so would implicate Carrie in the robbery of the mobster in Maine and possibly the man's killing even though Skeeter was solely responsible. Skeeter wasn't sure what happened to that investigation after he left. Had the U.S. Marshals and the FBI quietly swept that affair under the rug, or was it still an open case?

If Detective Kajal Reddy learned that Carrie Fenton already robbed one man, it would cement her belief that the Maine author could steal from Mason Freemantle. It would only be a hop, skip, and a jump from that to believing her capable of murder.

What were the best courses of action for him to take, then? He could locate Lorraine Bagley and find out the truth of how and why she was so quickly on the seventeenth floor. He could also help Detective Reddy consider other suspects. Or was this crime such a slam dunk that she would simply wrap the case up by arresting Carrie Fenton? In the fast-paced world of homicide detectives, Skeeter figured the latter was the most viable.

To begin dismantling the detective's case, he asked, "Did Lorraine see Otto with Carrie?"

The detective shook her head. "No."

"If you were committing a robbery of forty thousand, would you leave your partner behind holding the bag?"

"You might if you just killed a man."

Skeeter shook his head. "That's a lot of cash to walk away from, especially after a murder. If your theory of two people together is to work, Otto would have stayed behind with Carrie to make sure he got his cut. That goes double if he was the one who did the killing. And if that were true, then Lorraine would have seen them both because she called the cops, right?"

Detective Reddy inhaled slowly. She nodded as she did so. "You talk as if you have some experience with this type of thing. Where did you say you were from again?"

"Findlay, Ohio. You wrote it down."

"That I did. Maybe it was just Carrie Fenton that committed the crime. If she was committing a robbery that led to murder, it's not too far-fetched to think she might have stolen a monkey wrench."

"As a murder weapon? That's unlikely. A hammer would make more sense."

"Listen, Mr. Dursky, Lorraine Bagley immediately reported the body. She found the Fenton woman standing over Mr. Freemantle. The only thing that would have made it better is if the woman were holding the murder weapon." The detective frowned. "She wasn't, but it was across the room. We can explain that easily enough."

"But—"

The detective cut him off. "With the amount of evidence and witness testimony we have, it's like the whole thing was gift-wrapped for the

Chicago Police Department. An early Christmas present if you will. Since homicide cases are tough enough, I'm not going to thumb my nose at one that solves itself." Reddy shifted her stance and hooked her thumbs in her waistband. "You've known Otto Cantrell for a few days. If you were him, where would you be right now?"

"I honestly don't know."

She checked her watch. "It's almost noon. Does he eat lunch? I guess that doesn't matter. The kitchen is closed."

"Maybe he went for a walk."

"We locked down the building."

"Maybe he got out before it was."

The detective's nose twitched. "Maybe."

"Maybe Carrie Fenton made it out, too."

"We know she didn't. Her car is in the parking lot, and one of my men has an eye on it. No, that woman is still in the building. I can feel it. We've got more officers on the way. They're bringing a search and rescue dog, too. They'll sniff her out."

Skeeter's eyes moved to the body and the purse once more. "Do you need me for anything further?"

Reddy shook her head. "Stay out of trouble." She called down the hallway. "Metcalf, send him back down."

The officer relaxed as Skeeter approached and hit the call button. According to the floor counter, both elevators were currently on the third. That seemed an odd occurrence, but he seemed to be experiencing a number of those since arriving at the Lake Michigan Tower. Skeeter and Carrie Fenton being in the same place at the same time was living proof.

"I gotta thank you for those granola bars," Metcalf said. "They really hit the spot."

"I would imagine."

"Topped off the ol' engine, so to speak."

"Right."

Metcalf looked up at the floor counter. "What's taking the elevators so long?"

For the next several minutes, the two men made idle chatter. Mostly it was Metcalf blathering on about the dryness of other granola bars or the unhealthiness of candy bars, but Skeeter listened dutifully. What else was there to do when left alone with a cop? It was better to let them occupy the airspace than fill it with some of his own thoughts. That's when the police officer would start asking questions, and Skeeter wanted to avoid that scenario.

The cop entered a new phase of the conversation when he asked, "Who do you think first came up with the idea of mixing chocolate with granola? I mean, those are like crazy things to combine."

To avoid answering the question, Skeeter pointed at the floor counters. "They're still stuck on three. I'll take the stairs and see what the holdup is."

Metcalf shrugged. "It's all downhill from here." He chuckled at his joke.

Skeeter smiled politely and walked away. He shoved open the door marked *Stairwell* and began his descent.

Chapter 11

It took a few minutes for Skeeter to descend fourteen flights. When he stepped out onto the third floor, several residents stood in front of the elevators. Skeeter recognized one face in the small group.

Shirley Tilson moved from the first car to the second. She still wore the nicely pressed slacks and the bright yellow blouse she had on earlier. "What about this one?"

An older man with a flat-top haircut poked his head out of the furthest elevator. "Same as the other—fugazi."

"What's that?" Shirley asked.

A woman Skeeter assumed was the man's wife said, "Harold means it's not working." She wore a simple green dress with a white sweater over it.

Shirley said, "We can always take the stairs." She turned in the direction of the stairwell and saw the big man approaching. "Never mind. Skeeter's here."

The older man now stepped clear of the elevator. He wore a black polo shirt, khaki pants, and black boots. "Who?"

"Otto's assistant." Shirley pointed at Skeeter.

Harold crossed his arms. "He doesn't inspire much confidence when he moves like pond water."

Skeeter stopped and eyed the older man.

Harold eyed him right back. "Did I hurt your feelings, princess?"

He shook his head.

"Then what's with the impression of a stump? Got a part in a school play?"

Skeeter ground his teeth to avoid saying something he might regret.

Harold eyed Shirley Tilson. "You sure this one knows what he's doing?"

"Otto seems to like him."

"He looks like he can't tell the difference between a left-handed screwdriver and a right-handed one."

Harold's wife leaned toward him. "What's the difference?"

"Shush, Gladys. Let the boy answer."

Skeeter ignored the older man and stepped past the small group to get into the first elevator.

"Is Otto on the way?" Harold asked.

"No."

"Don't be snappy with me, boy. I was in the service."

His wife said, "He was, you know."

The older man thumped his chest. "Without me, the gears of war would have starved to death."

Skeeter knelt. The control panel door was open, and the elevator had been locked into place. It required a key to do such a thing, but the key was missing.

"Can you fix them?" Shirley asked.

"Why ask him?" Harold chuckled. "This is obviously above his pay grade. He's a mouth-breather. Otto's the man for this sort of thing."

Skeeter glowered at the older man as he moved into the second car.

"That stink eye might scare the ladies," Harold said, "but not me." He stepped into the elevator. "You hear me, kid?"

Harold hadn't expected an angry Skeeter to move back toward him. "Oops," the older man said and rushed out of the elevator.

Now alone, the big man knelt at the control panel. This was the car that went to the basement. The key with the yellow tag was missing. "Someone locked the elevators here."

"You figured that out all on your own?" Harold said from the hallway. "Geez, this kid is a real light bulb."

Shirley stepped into the car. "Can you unlock them?"

"Yeah," Gladys added. "We've got places to be."

Skeeter shook his head and stood. "You're going to have to take the stairs."

Harold laughed. "What'd I tell you? The kid's a soup sandwich. Let's go back to our place until Otto fixes it." He marched down the hallway.

The wife lingered behind a moment. "Don't take it personally. He's like this to everyone." Then she hurried after him.

Skeeter and Shirley remained silent until the couple disappeared into their unit. When the door shut, Shirley faced him.

"What's going on, Skeeter? It's not like the building to lock down both elevators."

"You haven't heard?"

Mrs. Tilson shook her head.

"Mason Freemantle has been murdered."

"Oh my!" She covered her mouth with her hand.

"And the police think Carrie did it."

Her eyes widened. "I think I need to sit down."

**

Shirley Tilson's apartment sat on the south side of the building and overlooked the city. Unfortunately, Skeeter couldn't stand at the window and take it all in. Instead, he brought Shirley up to speed on the famous author's murder. He was careful what he revealed about Carrie, though.

"Carrie couldn't have done that to Mason," Shirley said. "She's not that type of girl."

Skeeter hadn't mentioned the hundred thousand her granddaughter had stolen from a mobster. He also hadn't mentioned the cash she brought to the building or the amount remaining in her purse. Pulling that string would have led back to Pleasant Valley, his time there, and what he did to earn that experience.

He asked, "Where did you go after you left the dayroom? When I saw you with Carrie?"

"I went to find Lorraine. I wanted to know what happened with the room mix-up."

"Did you find her?"

Shirley shook her head. "I found Charlotte, though. And she checked the scheduling book. And you know what she found?"

"You had reserved the dayroom for the book club."

She gasped. "How did you know?"

"It was a guess."

"And a good one. Do you know what this means?"

"That Lorraine bumped you for Mason Freemantle."

"She bumped me for Mason. That's right. She did. Why would Lorraine do such a thing?"

Skeeter shrugged. "My guess is she was either having a relationship with Mason or had a crush on him."

Shirley reared back. "That's horrible. She's young enough to be his daughter."

"I'm only saying. She seemed to be taken with him."

Her face softened. "He was dashing, and he had a way with words. But gross is gross."

"Shirley, do you know why there was bad blood between Carrie and Mason?"

"I don't. The first I heard of it was when you saw it. I wish I knew what was going on."

"Where was Carrie when you talked with Charlotte?"

"I left Carrie in the lobby. I told her to wait there and that I'd be right back. When I returned, she was gone. There seemed to have been some commotion while I was away. Folks looked at me with a bit of side-eye, but no one came out and said anything. I ignored it and came home. I figured Carrie had grown tired of waiting, but she wasn't here."

Skeeter pieced together the timeline of events.

After he told Shirley and Carrie the news about not getting the dayroom, they left and had a brief conversation. Shirley went back to the manager's office, where she found Charlotte. Lorraine was elsewhere. Carrie had her altercation with Mason in the lobby, which several residents witnessed. She followed him onto the elevator.

Shirley then returned to the lobby to find her granddaughter gone. She then went to her apartment. While Shirley was doing that, Carrie rode the elevator up several levels with Mason Freemantle until he pushed her out onto one of the lower floors. When he did so, she dropped her purse, and the stolen money fell out. She had to spend time collecting the funds. When Carrie finished, she hopped the next elevator to the seventeenth floor to discover Mason dead in his apartment. Lorraine arrived immediately after that and called out that Carrie had murdered the famous author.

"Why didn't Carrie come here?" Shirley asked.

"The cops would learn why Carrie was visiting the tower and discover the link between you two. They would eventually look for her here. Carrie would have figured that and headed elsewhere."

Shirley's eyes narrowed. "It sounds like you know where she is."

"I might have an idea."

Mrs. Tilson stood. "Well then, let's go find her. I want to help my granddaughter."

"I'm not sure that's the best thing—"

But Shirley wasn't listening now. She was already in the hallway. Skeeter hurried after her. "Mrs. Tilson. *Shirley.*"

She passed the elevators. "We'll have to take the stairs." Shirley glanced over her shoulder. "Up or down?"

"Just wait, Mrs. Tilson. This isn't a smart idea—"

A face appeared in the stairwell window a moment before the door swung open. Detective Kajal Reddy stood there with a surprised look on her face. "Well, well, well. If it isn't Skeeter Dursky. What are you doing here? And who is this?"

Shirley stepped forward. "Shirley Tilson. And who are you?"

The detective introduced herself.

"Are you the one investigating Mason's murder?" Shirley asked. "Let me tell you something—my granddaughter had nothing to do with it."

The detective raised an eyebrow. "You're Carrie Fenton's grandmother?"

Mrs. Tilson admonishingly waggled her finger. "She's a good girl, Detective. She wouldn't do the things you're accusing her of."

Reddy's gaze shifted to Skeeter. "As soon as

we finished talking, you ran down to the next of kin? What's your deal, Dursky? You want to be a fly in my ointment?"

Skeeter most certainly did not. "When I was up on seventeen, I saw that the elevators were stuck on this floor. I came down to investigate."

"That's why I'm here, too. What'd you find?"

He motioned for her to follow and walked back toward the elevators. "They've been locked in place. A key is needed to do that."

Reddy stepped into the first car and examined the opened control panel. She looked back at Skeeter. "Do you have one of these keys?"

He shook his head. "It's my third day."

"What does that mean? They don't trust you?"

"They haven't trained me."

"On how to turn a key?"

"On how to disable an elevator."

"What's to know?" Reddy examined the control panel. "The instructions are printed here. Insert key. Turn to the right to stop. Turn the left to start. You're trained. Or can't you read?"

Skeeter stared at her.

The detective stepped into the hallway and moved to the second elevator. As she did so, Skeeter lost sight of her.

"So," Reddy said from inside the elevator, "where were you two headed?"

Neither Shirley nor Skeeter replied.

When the detective reappeared, she said, "Did you not hear my question?"

"We were going downstairs," Skeeter said, "to

see if the kitchen was open."

"I already told you it was closed." Reddy pulled her radio from her belt. She depressed the call button and said, "Baggiano."

A moment later, Officer Baggiano replied. *"Yes, ma'am?"*

"Are you finished interviewing the kitchen staff?"

"No, ma'am. Still working on it."

"Thank you." She put her radio back on her hip. With a smile, she said, "I saved you a trip down the stairs. I'm helpful that way."

Skeeter and Shirley looked at each other.

"And since I've just found Carrie Fenton's grandmother, I think now would be a perfect time for us to get to know each other. Can we step into your apartment, Mrs. Tilson? Maybe sit down and have a chat."

Shirley hesitatingly nodded.

The detective's gaze shifted to the big man. "And you, Skeeter Dursky, go about your business. And do me a favor—"

"I know. Stay out of trouble."

"Well, yeah. But figure out a way to restart the elevators. I don't want the crime scene techs lugging their equipment up to the seventeenth floor. Someone is going to have to carry the body down if they don't start running soon."

Skeeter headed toward the stairwell.

Chapter 12

Skeeter exited the stairwell into the east hallway where his apartment was. He briefly paused as he tried to figure out his next course of action.

He wanted to find Lorraine Bagley for various reasons. How was she so conveniently on the seventeenth floor after Carrie Fenton's discovery of Mason Freemantle's murder? What happened to the missing sixty thousand from Carrie's purse? If Lorraine took the money, she must have been involved in the murder. Her fast arrival certainly dictated it.

Didn't it?

Skeeter also wanted to find Otto Cantrell. He didn't know the man very well, but it seemed unlike the maintenance supervisor to suddenly disappear. Thinking about Otto made him remember that the man's radio somehow ended up in Carrie Fenton's purse.

Had Lorraine put it in there? That certainly seemed the most likely explanation. She took the radio from Otto and then put it in Carrie's purse to point blame at the older man.

His hand drifted to his radio. He'd left the volume down while with Detective Reddy. Skeeter turned it back up.

Should he call Lorraine now and request a location to meet? He hadn't called her at any time in his short time at the tower.

Would doing so now seem out of line?

Would she be suspicious of him doing so?

Skeeter lifted the radio to his mouth. There was a dead man in the building. If there was ever a time to break tower protocol, this would be it.

Pressing the microphone's button, he said, "Lorraine, this is Skeeter. Is there a place we can meet?"

His request was met by silence.

Since he was right next to his room, he decided to check his cell phone and see if Gayle Goodspeed had called. He didn't carry that item with him because he didn't want it to become too familiar. Doing so may allow it to become the thing his former witness inspector feared. In a moment of melancholy, Skeeter might be tempted to pull it from his pocket. Perhaps to call his grandmother. Maybe to hear the voice of Daphne Winterbourne. No, the cell phone needed to be an item he went to, so he would have a moment or two to reconsider any call he was about to make.

When Skeeter stepped inside his apartment, the cat didn't trill or chirrup. He didn't even run to him, which was a behavior the tom had quickly adopted in the small unit.

"Travis?" he called.

"In here," a woman said.

Instinctively, Skeeter hunched, but the female voice was cigarette-scarred and instantly recognizable. He relaxed and stepped around the corner. Seated on the edge of his bed was U.S. Marshal Gayle Goodspeed. She wore a heavy sweater, jeans, and running shoes. Travis lay contently in her lap as she ran her hand from head to tail.

"What's he doing?"

"Purring." She smiled at the tom. "That's some motor."

"He doesn't do that for me."

"Do you pet him?"

Skeeter's lip curled. "We have an agreement."

Goodspeed looked up. "Only you would have a cat that you won't pet."

"How'd you get in?"

"We have our ways."

"No, seriously. The building is locked down. Cops are watching every exit."

The marshal's gaze returned to the cat. "A marshal's badge carries a lot of weight."

"But a cop would report your entry up the chain of command."

"Not when career ambitions are at stake."

Skeeter smirked. Goodspeed had found an officer who wanted something the marshal could provide—either a leg up in his career or an eventual boost into the marshal service. Cops were as mercenary as outlaws.

"What's its name?" Goodspeed asked.

He didn't want to play the name-the-cat game with the marshal, so he said, "Travis."

She smiled and stroked him. "Named after Travis Tritt, no doubt."

Skeeter had no idea who that was.

"Or maybe Randy Travis?"

The second name made less sense than the first. The guy could have been the marshal's accountant for all he knew.

"Why am I here, Beau?"

"I've been made."

Goodspeed's gaze snapped to him. "You've been here three days."

"I can explain."

The marshal held up her hand. "How many covers have we built for you?"

"Four."

"And out of those four, how many are now blown?"

Skeeter remained silent.

Goodspeed's smile was humorless. "Right. And do you know what the common denominator is in all those scenarios?"

His shoulders slumped. "But I didn't do anything."

"Now, you want to play the victim?" Goodspeed scratched behind the cat's ear. "Are you ready?"

"Don't you want to hear my side of the story?"

"You said you've been made. I believe you. The first order of business is to get you safe."

"But there's been a murder."

Goodspeed cocked her head. "Who did you kill?"

"I didn't do it."

"Then what do we care? It's the locals' problem. Besides, the press is on the way, which is even more reason to get you out of here.

Remember what happened in California?"

Skeeter wasn't surprised she knew about the impending arrival of the press. He had learned not to question the intelligence resources of the U.S. Marshals.

He said, "I want to wait."

Goodspeed's hand settled gently onto the cat. Her voice softened into a whisper. "Don't make me upset this good boy. He's so content, and it's making me happy."

"Why would you upset him?"

"Because I'm about to yell, Little Sister."

He hated when she called him that. Not only did Skeeter dislike being called names, he especially despised it when he didn't understand what they meant.

The marshal continued. "We've spent a lot of time, money, and energy protecting you, and you can't seem to keep yourself out of trouble."

"I didn't do this to myself."

She repositioned the cat in her lap. "This should have been the perfect place for you."

"A retirement community?"

"Why not?" Goodspeed cast an unbelieving look his way. "There's not much surveillance equipment in the building. Or didn't you notice?"

"I noticed."

"Did you stop and ask yourself why? I'll tell you. It's because older folks aren't likely to steal from each other."

He thought about how he left his apartment unlocked. It was how Goodspeed had managed to enter his room. Maybe he should start locking it.

The marshal resumed petting the cat. "And how many cell phones have you seen?"

Besides his own, he'd seen a few. He imagined most of the residents had them, though. They just didn't constantly play with them.

"The residents don't run around pretending to be Instaface influencers." Goodspeed eyed him. "Do you know what that is? Instaface? I do."

Skeeter didn't, but he got the gist of it.

"These people have something called maturity, Beau. Senior citizens might be boring to someone of your background, but for a man looking to hide under the radar they're a safe bet."

"They don't like me."

"So what? I don't like you either. What's that got to do with the price of rice?"

"I thought there was a computer that spit out the perfect place to be hidden in."

"There is." She tapped her temple. "It's right here, and it said this was the place for you. Or was until you messed it up."

"That's what I'm trying to tell you. I didn't do anything. It was Carrie Fenton who showed up."

"Who?"

"I met her in Pleasant Valley."

"Which is a place you already messed up. The common denominator, remember. And somehow, this woman shows up here? Chicago isn't Cabot Cove."

"I don't know where that is."

"Oh, dear Lord. It's where *Murder, She Wrote* took place. That's a TV show."

He hadn't heard of it. He did know, however, that *Murder, She Wrote* was a book. He'd beaten a man over the head with a hardcover version once.

Goodspeed continued. "People don't just show up in a later episode, Beau."

"Her grandmother lives in the tower. Carrie's visiting. It's a simple explanation."

The marshal rolled her eyes. "And I'm sure everyone in the tower knows Carrie, and the cops already suspect her of the murder."

Skeeter's grin was sheepish.

The marshal waved her hand. "Cabot Cove. I rest my case."

"You're right."

Goodspeed's hand paused in mid-wave. "I am?"

"The cops think Carrie killed Mason Freemantle."

"Yeah, he's good. A little too much romance in his books for my tastes, though. Is that why your girlfriend killed him?"

"She's not my girlfriend, and she didn't kill Mason. At least, I don't think she did."

"You're not sure, and yet you still want to help her?"

He nodded.

"Why?"

"Why not?"

"Tell me why you want to help. I need to

know."

Skeeter broke eye contact for a moment before admitting, "She knows my name—my real name."

The marshal's eyes flared. "You said she wasn't your girlfriend."

"She's not."

"Maybe you two got a little cozy in Pleasant Valley? Maybe you spilled your guts in a moment of post-coital honesty?"

He thought about Daphne Winterbourne. She knew about some of his past now. "I wouldn't reveal any of that to Carrie."

"Then how's she know?"

"She found the mob's website for tracking informants."

Goodspeed stiffened. "You know about that, too?"

Skeeter nodded. "The guy you replaced told me about it."

"Did you see yourself on there?"

Another nod.

"Holy— well, that's got to be a sobering thing to discover. So, helping this woman is about self-preservation. That's something I can understand. It's not a flattering side of you, but it's understandable. Anything else I need to know?"

"Maybe it's the right thing to do."

She snickered. "Said the felon." Goodspeed lowered the cat to the floor then stood. Travis trilled and ran toward his food bowl. "This may come as a shock to you, Little Sister, but you're not the only witness I've got to worry about."

"I know that. You've probably got a binder full of us."

"I meant here." She pointed at the floor. "You're not the only one I've got to worry about now."

He *knew* it! Excitedly, he asked, "The government owns the building, doesn't it?"

Goodspeed's face pinched. "What? No. What's wrong with you?"

"Then who else is here?"

"If I tell you, then I'm not doing my job. Besides, I've already said too much by saying what I did. I'm only trying to make you aware that we need to get you out of here for your safety and the safety of others. So, let's double-time it."

"But what about Carrie?"

"Let her worry about herself."

He crossed his arms. Skeeter didn't know what course of action he could take to get the marshal's approval to stay. He set his jaw and furrowed his brow. It was the hard look he gave when he was the club's bookkeeper. Many a man had cracked because they knew what waited for them if they didn't.

Goodspeed rolled her eyes. "Don't mean-mug me, kid. I've been a marshal for as long as you've been alive, and I've been married three times. *And* I won every divorce. That face doesn't scare me."

If he relented, she won, so he simply held the glare.

The marshal sighed heavily. "Fine." She moved to the window and pulled the curtain to the side. "You see my car over there? I'm going to go out and eat my lunch. While I'm doing that, I'll start working on your relocation."

"Pick me a better name next time."

"What's wrong with Skeeter Davis? She was a queen of country music."

He eyed her.

The marshal frowned. "You've got one hour."

"Only an hour?"

"Or we can go now. That would make me happy."

"Make it ninety minutes."

She shook her head. "Fine. You walk outside this door in ninety minutes, or I'm coming to get you."

"Can I bring Carrie?"

Goodspeed dropped the curtain. "I'm not assisting anyone escape justice. If you want to help your girlfriend, that's up to you—"

"She's not my girlfriend.

"But don't try to rope me into anything illegal."

"What about your other witness?"

The marshal put her hands on her hips. "Maybe I'll alert them to what's going on."

"You're going to tell them about me?"

"Relax. I wouldn't tell them your real name. Besides, you're leaving, so what's the problem?"

"Well—"

Goodspeed stepped forward. "Maybe we're jeopardizing their safety so you can play footsy with this girlfriend of yours."

"I'm not playing footsy with her, and she's not my—"

The marshal stopped him by holding up her hand. "Yeah, yeah. You've already told me, but I bet she's pretty."

Skeeter couldn't deny Goodspeed's accusation, or it would seem as if he were trying to hide something. And he didn't want to tell the marshal about Daphne Winterbourne. His other witness inspector knew about her. The fewer people knew about his pining, the better.

He asked, "What if the other witness reports me to the cops?"

She smirked. "They won't. Trust me."

"But what if this other witness finds Carrie and turns her over to the cops?"

"Good Lord, Beau. Focus on what's important. Your cover is blown, and we need to go. "

If he left with Goodspeed now, the witness left behind wouldn't know about him. That meant Carrie would have to get out of this predicament on her own. How long could she hide in the basement without the risk of exposure? Eventually, she would have to come out. Or the cops would discover her.

However, if Skeeter stayed and Goodspeed alerted the other witness, maybe that person wouldn't care if he looked for Carrie. Or perhaps they would get actively involved in locating Carrie to get her out of the building. That was unlikely. Their involvement would be to expose her so the cops would leave the tower.

It was a tough decision, but Skeeter Dursky believed in action over inaction.

"I'm staying."

"It figures." Goodspeed headed toward the door. "You got ninety minutes."

"You're not going to tell me to stay out of trouble? Most everyone else has."

The marshal shook her head. "You've got more trouble than you know what to do with. Luck is what you need."

Chapter 13

When the door to his apartment shut, Skeeter was alone. He lifted the radio from his hip. He depressed the call button and said, "Lorraine, this is Skeeter. Hello?"

While he waited for a response, he moved to the window and pulled the curtain slightly to the side. Gayle Goodspeed ambled across the parking lot and climbed into her Chevy Impala. After she closed the door, the marshal lifted a cell phone to her ear.

Why had she told him about the other witness?

Was it to protect him? To protect them?

Or was it simply to mess with Skeeter so he would hurry up and leave.

Whatever it was, it worked. He let the curtain fall back into place.

Skeeter pressed the radio's transmit button again. "Lorraine, this is Skeeter. Is there a location we can meet?"

Another minute went by, so he tried Otto.

"Otto, this is Skeeter. Where are you?"

As soon as he spoke, he realized he'd just called the radio sitting in Carrie Fenton's purse.

The radio squawked. *"Skeeter, this is Charlotte. We still haven't been able to find Otto. And now I don't know where Lorraine is."*

"Where are you?"

"Outside the dayroom."

"Doing what?"

"You've got to see it to believe it."

He clipped the radio to his belt and eyed the cat. "You're on guard now."

Travis trilled.

"If anyone else comes in, eat them."

The tom flopped over to its side.

***

In the lobby, almost the entire crowd was on the interviewed side. Only one woman remained on the uncontacted side, and she seemed lonely. She looked with envy at her friends across the lobby. They didn't seem to notice as they loudly demanded to be released to their rooms and for the reopening of the kitchen.

Through the large south-facing windows, Skeeter saw a new concern. The press had arrived. News vehicles were parked on the sidewalk, and press members rushed toward the front of the building. This gaggle of reporters and photographers headed toward the officer guarding the front entry. He held one hand up in the internationally recognizable symbol for stop. The other hand pointed to an arriving caravan of shiny, black cars with flashing lights.

Skeeter didn't need to hang around to know who was in those unmarked vehicles. That would be the leaders of the police department. It was natural for them to arrive. A celebrity was murdered, and the press corps was assembling.

A photo opportunity wouldn't be far behind. In his previous life, Skeeter had seen many of these—always from a distance, though.

The cluster of reporters and camera operators ran toward the arriving members of the police leadership.

"Hey!" an elderly man called out. "That guy can get us some snacks."

Several people turned eagerly toward Skeeter. He tried to shush them, but it was too late.

Officer Baggiano hollered. "Hey, you! Dursky! Get over here."

The residents surrounding Skeeter groaned as he moved through them toward the cop.

Baggiano flipped his phone closed and slipped it back onto his belt. "Where've you been?"

"Detective Reddy wants me to figure out what's going on with the elevators." He pointed back at the closed doors. The floor counters were still stuck on three.

The sudden realization that there was a new problem to worry about swept through the assembled crowd. "The elevators" was a hushed refrain as folks moved to stare at the frozen floor counters.

Baggiano put his hands on his hips. By now, the other shirttail had slipped loose of his pants and hung over the front of his duty belt. He looked like a man who had spent a hard day at the factory and pulled the garment free the moment he walked through the door of his home.

The cop opened a new piece of gum and stuck it in his mouth. Skeeter didn't want to know what happened to the previous one. Baggiano motioned toward the elevators. "There a problem with them?"

"They're stuck on the same floor. The detective wants me to figure out how to get them started again, so the evidence team won't have to climb to the seventeenth floor."

The cop's nose scrunched, but he continued chomping on his gum. "Think about the coroner's boys lugging a body down that many flights."

"Exactly."

"If that's the case, what are you doing standing around here?"

"You called me over."

Baggiano waved his hand. "Do what the detective wants. Can't you see I'm busy?"

Outside the building, the assembled press swarmed a group of white-shirted police officers. One man lifted his hands, smiled, and began to speak.

If there was one thing Skeeter knew, nothing went well for him when the cops were around. It went even worse when the press was thrown into the mix.

***

Charlotte Olsen stood in the hallway just outside the dayroom. Her attention was focused intently on whatever was occurring inside the room.

When Skeeter moved next to her, she broke her trance. "Hey, there."

"What's going on?"

"Besides the cops at every exit?" Her gaze moved toward the end of the hallway. "I wonder how long that's going to last."

"Until they find Mason's killer."

Charlotte clucked her tongue. "Great."

"What did you want to show me?"

She pointed into the dayroom. "Take a look."

A group of women was seated on the chairs he'd set up earlier. All were openly weeping. Several clutched books to their chests. Skeeter recognized a few of them. In the morning, they had been with Shirley Tilson and had excitedly spoken with Mason when he left the elevator.

"The Freemantles," Skeeter said.

"Excuse me?"

"It's something the Ketterlings called the fans of Mason Freemantle."

Charlotte's lip curled. "The Freemantles." She lifted her chin to the crying women. "Don't you think they're a little old for this type of behavior? This is the type of thing teenagers do."

"Maybe it was because he lived here."

She shrugged. "I guess."

"You don't approve?"

"What I think doesn't matter. They can do what they want."

"Why aren't they with the group in the lobby?"

She eyed him. "Who are you—the hall monitor?"

"No, I—"

"Just teasing. I don't know why they aren't with the others. Maybe their grief got the better of them. What were you calling Lorraine for? Maybe I can help."

Skeeter didn't know if Charlotte might be the witness that Marshal Goodspeed had mentioned. Therefore, he couldn't come out and say that he suspected the building's manager of stealing Carrie Fenton's money. He also couldn't say he thought Lorraine might be responsible for Mason's death. He had to come up with some other plausible reason.

"The elevators are frozen."

Charlotte nodded. "I saw that. Crazy, huh?"

"The detective wants me to get them started. Do you have a key?"

She shook her head. "Only Lorraine and Otto. And the elevator company, of course."

"Of course."

"But they're not here."

Only the building's manager or its maintenance supervisor could have stopped the elevators—unless Charlotte was lying. The older man, Clancy, had said she fibbed when Skeeter denied his cat was blue. Did she have a propensity toward untruths? He hadn't seen it before, but it had only been three days.

He needed a question to see if she would deny it. "Did you talk with Shirley Tilson?"

"About the dayroom reservation?" She nodded. "It was clearly marked for her."

"So, Lorraine bumped her request for

Mason's?"

"You say that like you're surprised."

"You're not?"

"Lorraine was sweet on Mason."

"I thought it was more than a crush. He invited her to have some wine up in his apartment."

"The cad." Charlotte intently watched the women in the dayroom.

"Why do you say that?"

"He's invited us all at one time or another."

"Did you go?"

Her smile was sardonic. "Not if he was the last man on earth." Her gaze slid to Skeeter. "Besides, he didn't believe in astrology. Did we settle on what sign you were?"

"Where do you think Lorraine and Otto are now?"

Charlotte frowned. "Your guess is as good as mine." She turned her attention back to the women mourning the famous author. "But their silence on the radio seems suspicious. The two of them missing right after Mason Freemantle gets murdered leads to some nefarious thoughts."

"Do you think something happened to them?"

She shrugged. "Maybe. Maybe not. What if they were involved in Mason's murder? Did you ever think of that? And that's why they aren't responding."

Skeeter thought Lorraine could easily be involved, but Otto? The maintenance supervisor disliked the author and had threatened him when alone with Skeeter. Maybe it was possible they were both involved.

Charlotte shook her head. "Boy, the Freemantles are really going at it, aren't they? I love that term, by the way."

Inside the dayroom, the women huddled together and cried. It appeared as if they were recalling the stories in the books they held.

Charlotte eyed him. "You ever read his stuff?"

"No. Have you?"

"Not if he was the last writer on earth."

"I didn't know you had such a hatred toward him."

Charlotte turned to him. "It's not that. It's just that the women around here fawn over the guy. I've had enough of that. I'd rather read the back of a cereal box than one of his books. What are you going to do now?"

"Keep looking for Lorraine and Otto, I guess."

With a final glance at the Freemantles, she said, "I'll go with."

"You don't have to." Skeeter didn't want someone he didn't fully trust looking over his shoulder. He would have trusted Charlotte had the marshal not planted the seed of another protected witness in the building.

Again, he wondered if there was a real witness in the building or if Goodspeed had done it simply to hurry him along.

Charlotte stepped back from the dayroom. "What else am I going to do?" She again glanced down the hall to the officer standing guard. "It's like the world hit the pause button." Abruptly, she faced him. "But you and I can be a team and go find Lorraine and Otto. It'll be an adventure." She hooked her arm in his and started toward the lobby.

Skeeter was about to decline when the assistant manager stopped at the door to the basement.

"Let's check down here first," she said.

"I already did."

She yanked open the door. "Let's do it again." She smiled and motioned for him to go forward. "After you."

***

Skeeter and Charlotte spent several minutes searching the basement. Actually, Charlotte searched, and Skeeter pretended to search. Anytime Charlotte got near the rack of uniforms and the shelf of paint that Carrie Fenton had previously hidden behind, he made some comment to divert her attention. Then he tried to direct her from the room.

The entire time the assistant manager searched, she blathered about nonsensical stuff. After telling him she was from Albuquerque, New Mexico, she asked, "Where did you grow up?"

"Ohio."

"Huh. Did you go to college?"

"No."

"Interesting. What's your favorite color?"

Skeeter said, "Blue," even though it wasn't.

He thought she might key in on the name she'd given Travis, but she didn't. Earlier, he thought she might be interested in him in a romantic way, but the way she searched the basement gave him pause.

Charlotte seemed relentless in her hunt. The more she moved items to look behind them, the more convinced Skeeter was that she wasn't looking for Lorraine and Otto but rather searching for Carrie Fenton.

"What are you doing?" Skeeter finally asked.

"I thought they might be back there."

"Why wouldn't they have come out when we called their names?"

"Maybe they're incapacitated. Maybe they know something about Mason's killer, and he's done something with them."

"You mean he might have killed them, too?"

Charlotte hesitated as if thinking. "Yeah," she finally said, drawing the single syllable out. "That would make more sense than tying them up and gagging them."

That thought hadn't occurred to Skeeter until then. He only thought that Otto and Lorraine were missing, most likely hiding for some reason. The idea that a nefarious individual might be behind them not responding could also be a reasonable explanation.

Skeeter and Charlotte walked back into the central part of the basement.

He paused at a workbench. If Otto had a monkey wrench, this would likely have been where he kept it.

"Can someone hide behind here?" she asked.

Skeeter turned to see Charlotte pointing behind the shelf full of paint cans.

He stiffened. "I already checked."

"You did?" She moved toward the rack of uniforms and pushed the three hanging there to the side.

"I did," Skeeter said. "There was nothing back there but cobwebs."

"When did you check? I didn't see that."

"You were looking the other way."

She studied him. "I'm going to look again just to be sure."

Skeeter stepped toward her. "You don't need to do that. I'll do it."

Charlotte lifted a hand to stop him. "Why can't I do it?"

"Because there are spiders back there. Big, ugly ones."

"You want to protect me?" Her face brightened. "That's sweet, but I can handle a few bugs." She moved toward the shelf.

"No, wait. I'll do it."

"Seriously, it's no problem. It's like you don't want me to see what's behind there."

Skeeter remained silent. It was too late to do anything else. If Carrie jumped out now, Charlotte would see her. If the assistant manager looked behind the shelf, Carrie would be found. The only thing to do was to prepare for the fallout.

Charlotte leaned behind the shelf. "Where are all those spiders that you're trying to protect me from?"

The big man stiffened.

"Well?" Charlotte asked. "Where are they? It's clean as a whistle back here."

Skeeter moved to look behind the shelving unit. "I must have scared them away."

"You did, huh?"

If Carrie wasn't hiding back there, where could she have gone? They had just searched the basement's entirety, so she was no longer down there.

There were three ways out—the elevator and the two stairwells at the opposite ends. The elevator car was locked on the third floor, so Carrie couldn't have left using that. She must have fled the basement using one of the stairwells. Either of those could have taken her to the seventeenth floor.

The stairwells also led to the first-floor hallways. He couldn't imagine her going there, though. Each hallway had the lobby at one end and a cop guarding an exit at the opposite. Besides the three staff apartments and the manager's office, there weren't many other rooms in the hallways. The kitchen and the dayroom were on the first floor, of course. And there was a small laundry room in the event a resident's in-unit equipment stopped working. In his three days at the tower, he hadn't seen anyone use the laundry equipment.

His gaze settled on the three hanging uniforms. There had been four. One was missing.

Maybe Carrie was on the first floor—if she thought no one would recognize her. Heck, she could hide on any of the other floors. All she had to do was enter an unlocked apartment and wait until the cops left the building.

Charlotte put her hands on her hips. "Well, Lorraine and Otto aren't here. Where else could they be?"

He faced her. "Have you checked Lorraine's office?"

She smirked. "Why would Lorraine hide in her own office? That's the first place anyone would look."

"I haven't looked there."

Charlotte's face flattened. With some resignation, she said, "Let's go."

Chapter 14

When Skeeter and Charlotte emerged from the basement into the west hallway, the first thing both did was look toward the exit and the cop standing guard.

"Still there," the assistant manager said.

"Did you expect them to leave suddenly?"

She shrugged. "A girl can hope."

They both turned toward the lobby. There really wasn't any need to see what was going on there since the cacophony of elderly voices had grown louder. Charlotte craned her neck for a better view.

"They're turning angry."

"I get why." Skeeter moved toward Lorraine's office—it stood just off the stairwell. "There's no food, they can't go home, and the whole thing is being watched over by a dictatorial cop."

"Sounds terrible."

"It sounds like prison."

Her eyes widened. "Have you been?"

Skeeter stopped. Why was she asking? If Marshal Goodspeed already told her, she would know he'd been to prison. Wouldn't she? Unless she was the type of witness who needed protection because they did the right things from the start. Skeeter wished the marshal had never told him another witness was in the building.

He tried the doorknob to the manager's office. "It's locked."

"Nice way to ignore my question." Charlotte bumped him out of the way. "I've got it."

"You have a set of keys to Lorraine's office?"

"Why wouldn't I?" She pushed open the door and stepped inside. "Even though I don't have my own office, I have to watch over this place when she goes on vacation or leaves the property for something."

Skeeter followed her inside and closed the door behind them. "What about the elevator? Do you know how to stop and start it?"

"Sure. Insert a key and turn the switch. It's so simple a kid could do it."

"But you said you didn't know how."

Charlotte faced him. "That's not what I said. You asked if I had a key which I don't. Only Otto and Lorraine have them. I get hers when she leaves for an extended period, but one of those two is always supposed to be on site. And neither of them is in this office so this is another bust." A soft smile formed, and she moved closer to the big man. "But we're alone again."

Skeeter moved away from her and stepped behind the desk.

Charlotte's smile vanished. "What are you doing?"

His finger slid along the scheduling calendar until he landed on the square for that day. There was an entry for *Shirley Tilson—Dayroom* that had been lined through. Underneath it was written *M Freemantle*. The next day was completely open, but Lorraine had said Shirley would be unable to book the room.

Now, Skeeter scanned the calendar. All entries were written in ink. Whenever one was canceled, it was lined through.

"Are you verifying I told Shirley Tilson the truth? Because I did."

"I believe you."

"It sure looks like you're checking up on me." She put her hands on her hips. "I'm not a liar."

"I didn't say you were."

"This place is full of gossipers, so be careful with what you say."

"If you have to know," Skeeter said, "I'm checking up on Lorraine." He dropped into the manager's chair and opened the top desk drawer. In the corner, he noticed a key with a tag labeled *Master*.

"Now, what are you looking for?"

"Something."

Charlotte crossed her arms, and her hip jutted to the side. "You need a better reason than that."

Skeeter wasn't sure what he was looking for. It was unlikely that Lorraine would hide the missing money in her desk. Not when Charlotte had a key to the office. So, where would the manager put the stolen cash?

In the bottom drawer were a series of employment files. He saw everyone listed—Otto, Angel, Charlotte, and the entire kitchen staff. For a moment, he thought about pulling his own file. He wanted to know what records they kept on him. It was the same curiosity he had whenever he was around a police station.

Charlotte clucked. "You're violating Lorraine's personal space—not that I'm her biggest fan, but still. Personal space is important. I wouldn't want people sticking their noses into my business. Not that I have anything to hide."

His fingers walked themselves back to Charlotte's file. He lifted it from its resting place and had parted it. The only two things he saw were the name on her application—*Charlotte Thrasher-Olsen* and a handwritten note in the corner—*divorced.*

"You shouldn't be in those," she said. Charlotte moved around the desk. "Whose file is that?"

Skeeter pushed the file back into place and shoved the drawer closed. He noticed a file as the door banged closed. He pulled it back open and lifted the file out. On its tab was written *Bills.*

"What did you see?" Charlotte asked.

He laid it on the desk and flipped through the statements. Most were stamped with red-ink warnings such as 'second notice' or 'courtesy warning.' Among them were invoices for credit cards, utilities, and a car payment. The last piece of paper was a letter from a mortgage company with 'FINAL NOTICE' in bold type at the top.

Charlotte leaned over the desk. "Wow. Lorraine is far behind on her payments."

"Yeah," Skeeter muttered.

The assistant manager spread the letters apart. "Do you think she killed Mason because of this?"

"Why would she do that?" Skeeter asked.

"Didn't he have money?"

The big man turned to her. "She liked him, didn't she?"

"Maybe she was trying to extort him, and he didn't go for it. So, she killed him. That's motive, right?"

Charlotte couldn't have known about the cash in the purse, but she came very close to the thought that Skeeter had. The stack of bills showed the building's manager was in desperate need of money. Maybe she had tried to extort Mason Freemantle for something, but the author didn't have what she needed. She killed him, then Carrie Fenton's purse fell into her lap.

If that were true, why wouldn't Lorraine take the entire amount of money? The obvious answer was to create another suspect in the murder. But if she were that desperate, could she be disciplined enough to leave forty thousand behind? It was possible, but it seemed a slim likelihood.

Skeeter closed the file and tucked it back into the drawer. This time he carefully shut it. Now, he had a motive for why the manager took some of the money from Carrie's purse. But Lorraine's motive for murder seemed weak.

The question now became what was really in

Mason Freemantle's safe.

Detective Kajal Reddy believed the money in the purse came from there. Skeeter knew better, but he still needed to find where Lorraine hid the stolen cash to prove she was involved.

He looked up to Charlotte. "Is there someplace in the building that only Lorraine has access to? Someplace only she can keep something hidden?"

"It's a retirement community. Everyone leaves their doors unlocked. There are no secrets here."

His smile was without humor.

"What's so funny?"

Skeeter was about to reply when the door burst open. A sweaty and red-faced Lorraine Bagley stalked in.

"What are you doing behind my desk? Get out from behind there!"

***

"So, that's when we came here," Charlotte said.

Lorraine dabbed her face with a paper towel. Her pale skin glistened, and the underarms of her blouse were darkened with sweat. "You were looking for Otto?"

"And you," Charlotte added. The assistant manager looked to Skeeter who had remained mostly quiet during the retelling of the events that led them to this office. "Isn't that right, Skeeter?"

The big man nodded.

"What about Carrie Fenton?" Lorraine asked. "Has she been found?"

Skeeter shifted in the chair in front of the desk. "Not that we know of. The radio's been silent since you and Otto went missing."

"I wasn't missing." Lorraine reached to her hip. A very audible click was heard.

"Was that your radio?" Skeeter asked.

The manager's face pinched. "Excuse me?"

"Did you just turn on your radio?" He cast a sideways glance to Charlotte. "I was told it was a violation of policy to turn off our radios. Seems doubly so following the death of a celebrity resident."

Lorraine leaned forward. Anger flashed in her eyes. "Are you questioning me? I'm the manager."

Charlotte waved a hand to catch Lorraine's attention. "That's not what he was doing. I think he just—"

"Yes," Skeeter interrupted. "That's exactly what I was doing."

There was nothing to lose now. Gayle Goodspeed was outside waiting for him to wrap this up. He started with ninety minutes to find Mason Freemantle's killer and clear Carrie Fenton. He had less than that now. Skeeter was becoming more confident that Lorraine Bagley was behind it all. Being nice now would only slow things down.

He continued. "I want to know why you turned your radio off, I want to know where you've been, and I want to know why you're so sweaty."

"You want?" Lorraine stood. "I won't stand for this insubordinate behavior."

Skeeter raised an eyebrow.

The manager glanced at her assistant. "From either of you."

Charlotte's eyes widened. "What did I do?"

"You're with him." Lorraine pointed at the big man. "He's making insinuations, and I don't like it."

"He's not insinuating—" Charlotte began.

The manager's face pinched. "Out!" Her extended finger moved to the door. "Both of you, get out of my office."

Reluctantly, Charlotte stepped toward the door, but Skeeter didn't move.

"The elevators are stopped," he said.

"Call Otto," Lorraine snapped.

"We've tried." Charlotte lifted her hands in frustration. "We can't find him."

Skeeter crossed one leg over the other. "And you know his radio is at the crime scene. You even told Detective Reddy it belonged to him."

Lorraine swallowed with some difficulty. "Right. That's right." She touched her head and sat again. "This day has me discombobulated. I'm all turned around."

Skeeter was about to call her out on that statement, but he had tried to reach Otto on the radio himself. Was her gaff enough to accuse her of a crime when he'd made a similar one? No. He needed more proof.

Charlotte put her hands on the back of her chair and leaned toward Lorraine with mild excitement. "Otto's radio is at the crime scene? Do you think he killed Mason?"

"Maybe," Lorraine said. "There's some additional evidence that he could be involved."

"What kind?" Charlotte asked.

Lorraine relaxed and leaned back in her chair. "They found a bloody monkey wrench."

"Are you for real?" Charlotte turned and stared at Skeeter. "Otto finally went through with it."

"What do you mean *finally*?" Skeeter asked.

"He hated Mason. He said it all the time. I definitely heard him say it. How about you, Lorraine?"

The manager nodded.

"What about you, Skeeter?" Charlotte asked. "Did you ever him say it?"

He ignored the question. "The cops don't think he was working alone. They think Carrie Fenton is involved." Skeeter turned to Lorraine. "Isn't that right?"

The manager's eyes narrowed. "Why are you looking at me? She was in there when I arrived. Leaning over the body like she'd just killed the man. I did what I could to stop her."

"You grabbed her purse."

"How else would I stop her? I'm not going to tackle the woman. She just killed a man. Think about what she might have done to me. How do you know so much about this?"

"Then you called the cops."

Lorraine's face hardened. "That's right. That's what I did. And I think I told you two to get out of my office."

"The elevators are stopped," Skeeter reminded her again. "Detective Reddy wants them started. You're the only one around with a key."

The manager's face relaxed. "I don't have it anymore."

"You lost it?"

"Is that what I said? No. That's not even close to what I said."

"If you didn't lose it, where's it at?"

"What's with the twenty questions?" Lorraine wiped her sweaty forehead. "I put my key into elevator two, so others couldn't call it. That way, the cops would be able to control it, and now it's missing. Obviously, someone took it."

"With Otto missing," Skeeter said, "now no one has a key."

"That's the way it looks," Lorraine said. "What's with you playing detective? Did you join the Chicago PD while I wasn't looking?"

Charlotte watched him.

"No," Skeeter said. "I'm just wondering what's going on."

"There's been a murder," Lorraine said. "What else is there to know? I'll call the elevator company and get them started. Why do I have to do everything?"

"Because we can't find Otto," Charlotte reminded. "Probably because he killed Mason Freemantle and is hiding out with that author lady."

Skeeter stood. "I don't think so. Maybe something happened to him. What do you think, Lorraine?"

"There's that tone again. Are you accusing me of something, Skeeter?" She eyed the big man. "For someone only on the job three days, maybe you should hold your tongue."

He left the office.

***

In the hallway, Charlotte said, "Hey, wait up."

Skeeter didn't slow, though. He was on a mission, and the clock was ticking.

The crowd in the lobby was in an uproar now. There were no divisions between those interviewed and those waiting to be. It was a mass of gray hair surrounding one overwhelmed cop.

Officer Baggiano helplessly waved his hands in the air. "Go back to your apartments," he hollered. "Go back."

"And take the stairs?" one resident shouted.

"Let's tell the press," another suggested.

"Yeah!" a group hollered in support.

"Make lunch, not war!" someone offered. The kitchen staff quickly joined that chant.

When he passed by the elevators, the automatic dispenser blasted a whiff of the cinnamon and pumpkin scent. Skeeter waved the fake Thanksgiving smell away.

The assistant manager asked, "Where are we

going?"

He didn't answer and had almost made it to the east hallway when Clancy stepped in front of them to block their path. The older man lifted his cane with the four balls on each foot. It dangled in the air as he spoke. "Just where do you two think you're going in such a dadburn hurry?"

"The laundry room," Skeeter said.

The older man's eyes narrowed. "You're choosing to wash your delicates during this state of emergency? You millenniums have the worst sense of entitlement. My granddaughter—"

Skeeter stepped around the older man and pressed on.

"You know what?" Clancy bellowed after him. "You're as rude as a burp in church!"

Charlotte trotted up to Skeeter. "That's not very good customer service. Don't worry, though. I won't say anything about it."

"I'm not worried."

"Yeah?" She smiled at him. "You're over this job?"

"I'm running out of time."

"Got a hot date?"

"Something like that."

He burst into the laundry room. It was brightly lit and smelled of Pine-Sol and lint. The small facility only had five washers and five dryers. The only ones to regularly use the equipment were the kitchen staff, and they seemed to use it for dish towels. The linens for the tables were sent out, and each resident had a washer/dryer combo in their unit.

Charlotte sighed. "We should give up. Otto and Shirley's granddaughter probably left the building."

"They couldn't have." Skeeter pushed by her on the way out of the room. "Well, she couldn't have."

"How do you know that? Now, where are you going?"

He crossed through the hallway into the kitchen. It seemed odd to be in the room without the staff.

"They're not going to be here," Charlotte said. "And how do you know that about Shirley's granddaughter?"

Skeeter continued his search by opening every door but found only a pantry, a mop sink, and a small break room for the staff. He then entered the cooler.

"Do you know where that Fenton lady is hiding?"

"No," he said over his shoulder.

"Well, they couldn't hide in there for long," Charlotte said. "Unless they snuggled, but Otto doesn't seem the type. I don't know about the woman. Do you know her?"

Skeeter ignored the question and continued looking. The cooler was stocked with items like vegetables, milk, and other sundries. Next, he moved toward the freezer.

The assistant manager didn't enter with him but offered, "They would last even less time in there no matter how much they canoodled." She giggled. "Canoodled. I like that word. What about you?"

He stopped and looked over his shoulder. "Are you going to help?"

"Not in there. It's too cold. Besides, you're doing fine, and my view is better from back here."

Skeeter glanced back, and Charlotte seemed slightly embarrassed. She didn't look away, though.

He opened the freezer and entered. It didn't take long for him to confirm that no one hid inside. He slammed the door closed.

After rubbing his hands for warmth, Skeeter closed his eyes and rubbed his face. What happened to Otto Cantrell, and where had Carrie Fenton run off to?

"What are you thinking?" Charlotte asked.

"Where else could they be?"

"What about the dining hall?" she offered.

It was a wide-open room off the lobby and open to the public.

"They wouldn't be there. Everyone would have seen them."

"How do you know? Have you checked? I know I haven't." She gave him the same look he gave her when he asked about the manager's office.

Lorraine, he thought. "Why was Lorraine so sweaty?"

"I don't know. Could she have been working out?"

"At a time like this?"

"Maybe she was in a fight."

Skeeter shook his head. He'd been in plenty of scraps and had seen others involved in them as well. Lorraine didn't have a bump or bruise on her. She only looked sweaty. "No. She wasn't in a fight."

"Then why is exercising out of the question?"

The weight room was on the second floor. With the elevators out, he'd have to take—

"The stairs," he said. "She's sweaty because she used the stairs."

Charlotte nodded. "That makes sense. You're pretty good at this."

"She wouldn't have gotten sweaty going up a single flight of stairs."

"I don't know. Maybe if she did it in a hurry."

"It's not likely, but if she walked all the way up to the seventeenth floor to talk with the detective, that might explain it."

"But what would she want to say that was so important?"

"I don't know."

"You can always go up there yourself and find out."

He'd pass on that suggestion. Detective Kajal Reddy seemed like a capable investigator, but walking up the entire length of a building to ask her a couple of questions didn't sound enticing—especially not when the clock was ticking until Goodspeed insisted he leave.

Skeeter could call the detective on Otto's radio, but that would mean Lorraine could overhear it. No, he needed to be smart about this. Before he walked up to the seventeenth floor, he needed to be sure he'd checked everything else below it.

Even though he didn't think Lorraine had worked out in the fitness room, he hadn't checked out any second-floor rooms. "Let's go up to the next floor."

Charlotte pointed toward the lobby. "Why don't we check out the dining hall instead? It'll only take a minute."

He looked up at the clock on the wall. He didn't have minutes to waste, and he didn't want to walk through the lobby again. "You go to the dining room, and I'll head up to the second floor."

Charlotte put her hands on her hips and thrust her chin out. "We should stay together. We're adventure buddies."

"Adventure buddies?"

"You know." She winked. "Dining room first. Then we'll go to the exercise facility together."

Even for Charlotte, it seemed overly flirtatious at a time like this. Skeeter's first thought went to the other witness hiding in the building. If Marshal Goodspeed had simply made up the story as a ploy to hurry him along, then Charlotte's overtures were a signal that something was off. He'd met several women like that during his time with the Satan's Dawgs and actually enjoyed their company. But he wasn't after that sort of thing now.

However, if Charlotte were in the Witness

Protection Program, then a more subtle approach was needed for them to get on equal footing.

Skeeter said, "I know."

Charlotte's eyes widened.

"It wasn't hard to figure out."

Now, her brow furrowed. "What gave it away?"

"You know who."

She blinked. "Who?"

He raised his eyebrows.

A small smile hinted at the corner of her lips. "I guess I wasn't doing a good job of keeping it a secret. Was I?"

"I'm surprised they put us here together. It seems totally against protocol."

Charlotte's face scrunched. "Protocol? And who are they? You mean Lorraine?"

Skeeter straightened.

Charlotte moved closer. "You talk funny sometimes." She tried to slide her arms around him, but Skeeter pushed her back. "But they say that about bad boys." She suddenly appeared sleepy. "You're a bad boy, aren't you?" Her voice lowered an octave. "I can tell. Does this mean we're going to be more than adventure buddies?"

He pushed her away. "I think it's better if you check the dining hall and I check the weight room."

Charlotte pouted. "Playing hard to get?"

"I just think it's smarter this way."

"Fine. We'll do it your way." She patted the radio on her hip. "I'll call you when I get done and meet you up there. Keep your radio on this time."

She headed for the kitchen's exit. Before she stepped into the hallway, Charlotte looked back. It appeared as if she wanted to say something else, but she settled on, "I like your cat."

When she left for the lobby, Skeeter made for the stairwell.

Chapter 15

Skeeter burst into the east hallway of the second floor and trotted for the exercise room. There were no apartments on this level—all rooms on this floor were aimed at providing a better quality of life for the residents.

No one was in the fitness center. Over the radio, "Something's Gotta Give" by Sammy Davis Jr. softly played.

On the far side of the room were two doors for the restrooms. The fitness center didn't have locker rooms. The residents were expected to change and shower in their units. These bathrooms were simply for those moments when a person needed a quick break. He hurried by three treadmills, two stationary bikes, and a Universal machine that provided an untold variety of workout options. Skeeter imagined no one was in either the Men's or the Women's restrooms, but he knocked and announced, "Maintenance," before opening each door. Both were empty.

Skeeter then crossed the hall and checked the craft room. It was an ample space with long folding tables set in parallel rows. Along each wall were shelving units stacked with bundles of cloths. They appeared to be sorted by color and texture. No one was there, either. He turned and trotted from the room.

There was no lobby on the second floor as it only served to be additional ceiling height for the first floor. He stopped at the edge of the hallway and looked down. From where he stood, he could see Charlotte Olsen leaving the dining room with Officer Baggiano. He seemed to be asking her very intent questions. She nodded and answered, almost seeming to enjoy the cop's sudden interest.

Skeeter wanted to keep watching the two, but time was at a premium. He had to go now.

Pressing himself against the wall with the elevators, Skeeter hurried to the west hallway. He kept an eye on the crowd below the entire time, with particular attention paid to the assistant manager and the overweight cop.

When he made it to the other hallway, he relaxed. From the ground floor, three faces looked up at him—Clancy, Muriel, and Edna. All of them motioned for him to come back down.

Skeeter turned and entered the hallway.

Charlotte conversing with Officer Baggiano bothered him. He didn't trust anyone making nice with law enforcement. His attitude might have softened somewhat because of recent interactions with the FBI agent and his former witness inspector, but cops were cops. They took away a person's freedom. Then they put them in jail and blamed everything on the citizen. Things could be going just fine for a guy until the law showed up with their shiny badges and jingly handcuffs. Maybe Skeeter should take some blame for how things turned out in his life, but if a cop hadn't been involved, he wouldn't be in the predicament he found himself in now.

Then again, he wouldn't have met Daphne Winterbourne.

He shook those thoughts from his head and checked the first door he came to—the salon. It was locked. Anytime Skeeter ran into a locked door in the Lake Michigan Tower, it surprised him. However, this was a rented space and, according to Otto, the stylist who ran this little business was on vacation this week. She would likely lock the door because she wasn't part of the community. The stylist was scheduled to return the following Monday.

Skeeter initially thought it a strange arrangement for a stylist to cater to the elderly, but he now saw how it could be a lucrative business. Most of the tower's residents never left the building. Many services were either provided on-site or were delivered directly to them.

For example, a laundry service picked up and delivered twice a week. And those residents who wanted a livelier gambling experience than the tower's weekly bingo game were escorted in comfort both ways courtesy of a van sent by the local casino.

Getting old had some perks, although Skeeter wasn't in a hurry to take advantage of them.

Next door—the entertainment room was open as expected. This room was used for movie nights and big events. Chicago sports paraphernalia lined the walls. White Sox and Cubs banners hung prominently. A Bears football helmet sat in a place of honor on a high shelf. A goalie's helmet with a Blackhawks' logo sat upside down on a table with napkins stuffed inside. But no one was inside.

That left only one room to check—the internet room or, as the plaque on the outside identified it, Community Computers. The Lake Michigan Tower maintained a state-of-the-art technology room. For a couple of hours each week, an intern from Loyola University came in and worked with the residents.

There was no intern in there now, though, and no residents.

Otto Cantrell thought the computer room a waste of time, and so did Skeeter. It was one of the few things the two men agreed upon—that computers were a misuse of space. In Skeeter's previous life, a club prospect or one of the hang-around girls handled the computer-related tasks the Dawgs needed. The only reason Skeeter now took an interest in computers was because of the mob's website for tracking informants.

This was the first time he'd been alone in the room since his arrival.

He tapped the keyboard of a computer to awaken it. After the screen came to life, Skeeter used two fingers and entered thefbiisabunchofdirtyrats.com.

When it asked for a username and password, he entered those his original witness inspector provided him.

The screen changed and displayed: FBI RATS.

Skeeter swallowed. He'd only seen the site a couple of times, but each made his stomach churn. He hated being labeled a rat, but it was a title he'd earned.

He typed in his name—his real name.

A new screen popped up showing the information for Beauregard Smith.

Below that were various pictures of him during his time with the Dawgs. Following that were an artist's renderings of what he might look like with various hairstyles and colorings. Seeing a picture of himself bald and another with blond hair made him smile.

It was the information at the bottom of the screen that gave him pause. There were actual photographs from his recent sightings and where they were taken.

Pleasant Valley, Maine.

Costa Buena, California.

Belfry, Oregon.

No entries had been made since his recent arrival. No one knew he was in Chicago. He logged out and stepped into the hallway.

He felt certain that Carrie Fenton and Otto Cantrell were not on the second floor.

And Lorraine hadn't gotten sweaty walking to the second floor. Maybe she had climbed to the top of the tower like Skeeter had thought. If she didn't go to the top of the building to talk to Detective Reddy, what other reason would she have? An idea formed, and Skeeter ran for the stairwell.

He burst through the door and climbed the stairs two at a time. That only lasted for a few floors, though and his energy rapidly diminished. Soon, he was clomping his way up the remaining ten flights.

His legs burned, and near the top, he gulped for deep breaths of air. Skeeter liked to think himself a man in shape, but he hadn't trained to ascend a building such as this.

When he got to the seventeenth floor—the top, there was still another half-flight of stairs to the ladder that allowed roof access. However, he paused long enough to peer through the little window in the door. Officer Metcalf stood outside Mason Freemantle's apartment and appeared to be talking to someone inside. Even though he couldn't see her, Skeeter surmised it was Detective Kajal Reddy.

The radio on his hip squawked.

"*Skeeter,*" Charlotte called. "*Are you there?*"

Quickly, he deactivated the device. It wasn't fast enough since Officer Metcalf turned in his direction. Skeeter moved away from the window. Even though his legs burned, he ascended the remaining steps until he got to a small landing and a metal ladder affixed to the wall.

Above him was the roof hatch. He'd only been up there once on his first day when Otto toured him through the building. There'd been no reason to return since that day. Skeeter climbed the ladder only to discover a padlock on the hasp.

Half a floor below, the hallway door opened, and Officer Metcalf stepped into the landing. Skeeter froze on the ladder. The door clicked closed behind the cop.

"Anyone out here?" Metcalf asked. It sounded as if he moved about for a few moments. Eventually, he muttered, "Must be losing my mind."

Now, it sounded as if the cop was coming up the stairs to the roof hatch.

The hallway door opened again. Detective Reddy's voice now. "Metcalf, what are you doing?"

"I thought I heard something."

"Well? Did you find anything?"

"No."

"Then go downstairs and locate the other maintenance man."

"Skeeter?"

"That's the only one I know of. I want answers on why those elevators still aren't running. The forensic unit just arrived, and they're already complaining about climbing the stairs."

"Why not call Baggiano?"

"Because I'm asking you. Baggiano's already got his hands full down there."

"Couldn't we call Skeeter with the radio in the dead man's apartment?" There was a long pause until Metcalf reluctantly said, "It's evidence. Right. I'm on it."

There was stomping on the stairs now.

"And Metcalf," Reddy called. "Reopen the

kitchen. Let's get those people fed before there's a mutiny on our hands."

"Yes, ma'am."

"And I just got off the phone with the captain. He's going to send more cops in to do an apartment-by-apartment search for Carrie Fenton. Coordinate that with Baggiano."

"Won't we need warrants?"

"Tell everyone to ask nicely. Let's catch this Fenton gal and stick a fork in it."

The footfalls on the stairwell started again, and the hallway door closed. Skeeter stayed on the ladder for several minutes until he heard a door faintly open and close seventeen floors below. When he was sure he was alone, he jerked several times on the padlock. It wouldn't give.

He'd taken one step down when there was a loud crash on top of the hatch. It startled him so much, he let go of the ladder and fell several feet to the floor below. Skeeter lay sprawled on the concrete floor as another bang occurred above.

Slowly, he righted himself. No longer surprised by the banging, he climbed the ladder again and hammered his fist on the underside of the hatch—once, twice, three times.

The banging on the other side stopped.

"Hello?" a barely audible voice came from the other side.

"Otto?"

"Hello?"

Skeeter was sure the voice belonged to the

maintenance supervisor, but how did the man get himself stuck in this predicament. "Who locked you up there?"

"If someone is there, I can barely hear you."

When Skeeter had been on the roof, it had been noisy, windy, and cold. It was one of the realities of being that high up, outside, and on the shore of Lake Michigan.

"Let me in!" It seemed as if Otto was hollering, yet Skeeter could barely understand the man.

The big man didn't have a key for the padlock, so there wasn't much more to do. He'd have to run down to the basement and find a pair of bolt cutters—*if* the building had a set of bolt cutters.

"Hang in there," he muttered.

As he started down the ladder, another bang on the hatch surprised him, and his grip slipped. He fell the rest of the way but landed on his feet this time.

He started to take a step but paused.

Otto had been missing since Skeeter learned of Mason Freemantle's murder. Yet his radio was inside Carrie Fenton's purse. Skeeter suspected Lorraine Bagley had taken it and locked him outside on the roof.

How did she get his radio? How did she convince Otto to go on the roof before her? Why would he do that without his radio?

The maintenance supervisor banged on the roof hatch again. If he continued to do that, sooner or later, someone was going to hear it. Was that a bad thing? Shouldn't Skeeter just alert everyone to where he was?

No, he decided. Not yet.

He couldn't go to Detective Kajal Reddy about Otto's location. If he did so, she would likely grab the maintenance supervisor. With his radio in Carrie's purse, the detective suspected him as an accomplice.

But if Detective Reddy grabbed Otto, at least he would be off the roof. Would that be safer than where he was now?

No, Skeeter thought. At least for the moment, the maintenance supervisor should be left alone. He might be chilly, but he was safe and out of the way.

Then what should Skeeter do besides getting Otto immediately off the roof? He only had one other task—find Carrie Fenton. Nothing else mattered.

Skeeter descended the Lake Michigan Towers. As he jumped the stairs two at a time, he wondered how much time was left before Marshal Goodspeed forced him to leave.

Chapter 16

Skeeter pulled open the door to the third-floor hallway and stepped in. At the elevator stood Harold and Gladys, the couple he'd seen earlier. The older man still wore his black polo shirt, khaki pants, and black boots. However, his wife had changed into a simple red dress. She still wore the white sweater over it, though.

Harold turned expectantly to Skeeter but quickly threw his hands into the air. "Aw, heck, it's not Otto."

"Definitely not Otto." His wife shook her head.

As Skeeter trotted down the hallway, a grin creased the older man's face. "Now you're getting it, boy. Double time. Hup two, Hup two."

The wife watched Skeeter run by. "He looks like you did, honey."

"I did it with more style."

"He sure does sweat a lot."

Skeeter stopped at Shirley Tilson's door and knocked. The big man eyed the two at the elevator.

The older man faced him. "Hey, Not Otto. Got any idea when they're going to fix these?"

"Gonna be some time."

"Bah. Otto would have had it fixed by now." The older man grabbed his wife by the hand. "Let's go."

"We can take the stairs," the wife offered.

"And let them get away with this?" the man said. "What are we paying them for?"

They passed Skeeter on the way back to their apartment.

He knocked again and said, "Shirley, open up. It's me. Skeeter."

After a minute, the door cracked open slightly. "Yes?"

"Is she here?"

Mrs. Tilson affected a confused look. "Is who here?"

Skeeter whispered, "Carrie."

Shirley tried to look down the hallway, but she didn't poke her head out the door. "I don't know where she is."

"May I come in?"

Mrs. Tilson's gaze drifted back into her apartment. "There's no reason for you—"

"Shirley," Skeeter interrupted. His eyes narrowed. "I know she's in there. There's nowhere else she could have gone."

The older woman set her jaw. "Maybe she left."

"Every entrance is blocked by a cop. There's a bunch of reporters in the parking lot. Soon, there's going to be more cops here. They're going to go apartment by apartment searching for her. They'll find her here even if they have to get a warrant."

Her eyes darted about. "Have you checked the dining facility?"

"They would have found her."

Shirley's gaze still hadn't found a landing

point. "Maybe she's—"

From deeper inside the apartment came a woman's voice. "Let him in, Nana."

Shirley sighed and reluctantly stepped back.

Carrie Fenton stood in the doorway of a bedroom. She wore an ill-fitting drab-green uniform. The shirt was buttoned up to her neck, and the pant legs were rolled up around her ankles. Her long hair was hastily tied up, and loose strands hung in all directions. She appeared like a little girl wearing her father's work clothes. It called more attention than helped to hide her.

"What are you doing here?" she asked.

"Looking for you just like the cops. Sooner or later, they're going to find you. Why would you come here?"

"I didn't know where else to go."

"But you were smart to not come here at first."

Her eyes bulged. "Maybe I'm still freaking out. I'm not experienced at this sort of thing."

Shirley joined them now and rubbed her granddaughter's back. "It's okay, honey. We'll figure this out."

Carrie sighed. "How do you stay calm in situations like this? It's hard to think straight."

Skeeter leaned in. "Let me help you out. You're the prime suspect. The cops think you killed Mason Freemantle. Your purse is laying right next to Mason Freemantle's body."

Shirley inhaled sharply and covered her mouth.

Carrie muttered, "Crud."

"They think you have an accomplice, too."

"Who do I know here beside you and Nana?"

"Otto Cantrell."

Shirley spoke through her fingers. "Otto?

"The maintenance guy?" Carrie said.

Skeeter nodded. "They found his radio in your purse, and a monkey wrench was used as the murder weapon."

"Who uses a monkey wrench to kill someone?" Carrie asked.

"They think a maintenance man would."

"What's our motive?"

Skeeter said, "According to the detective, there was an open safe."

Shirley barked a short laugh. "If somebody was after money, I bet they got a real surprise. Mason doesn't keep anything in that safe but finished manuscripts."

"How do you know that?" Skeeter asked.

"It's common knowledge. Every Mason Freemantle fan knows that. You see, Mason never uses a computer. He works on an IBM Selectric." Shirley's fingers danced in the air. "It's a typewriter. Clickety-clack. There's something romantic about writing a novel on one of those. Don't you think?"

"Nana," Carrie said.

"I'm sorry, I do. Anyway, whenever Mason finished his pages, he put them into the safe. Just in case anything were to happen. A fire or whatnot. He kept them in there until it was complete. He told us this morning he finished his latest manuscript and that his agent would be by next week for it. Do you think the killer was after that?"

Skeeter eyed Carrie. "The cops think there was money in the safe."

"Money?" Shirley said. "Why would they think that?"

He kept his gaze on Carrie. "It would be a pretty big *purse* for any thief to score."

Her eyes widened, and she turned to her grandmother. Carrie grabbed Shirley by the shoulders. "Nana, would you sit for a minute?"

"Why?"

"I need to talk with Beau in private."

"Beau?"

Carrie glanced over her shoulder. "I mean Skeeter."

"He's your beau?" Shirley appeared confused. "I thought you two barely knew each other."

The author moved next to Skeeter and slipped her arm through his. "He fixed my car, remember?"

"But—"

"And he did such a wonderful job that I fell for him."

"This is awfully fast." Mrs. Tilson's face pickled. "What did he do again?"

"I fixed her carburetor," Skeeter said.

Carrie frowned at the big man before turning back to her grandmother. "He did a nice job. It really got my motor running."

"I don't know. That seems a terribly odd reason to fall for a man."

"Is that so, Nana? What attracted you to Papa?"

Mrs. Tilson's gaze took on a faraway look. "The way he did the Twist. He was something to see." She mimed the dance move while seated. "He was so handsome."

"That's what Skeeter looked like with a socket wrench."

Shirley raised a single eyebrow. "He did?"

"Show her." Carrie nudged Skeeter's shoulder with her own.

"What?"

Carrie's eyes widened. When she spoke, her voice was softer but still demanding. "Show Nana how you moved the socket wrench."

"No."

"*Do it.*"

Shirley leaned forward and watched the two with intense interest.

Reluctantly, the big man pantomimed the back-and-forth action of a socket wrench.

"Put your hips into it," Carrie said.

Skeeter glared at her as he continued to move his hands. Now, his waist began to undulate.

"Swing your hips more," the author said. "Really grease them up."

"I am," Skeeter growled. His body swayed more now.

"And move your hands. Like this." Carrie did the Twist now.

"Isn't that what I'm doing?"

Carrie shook her head. "It looks like you're driving a bus."

Skeeter stopped moving.

Mrs. Tilson shrugged. "I don't see it, but you two fight like you're in love."

"We are." Carrie tugged on Skeeter, and he stepped closer to her. "We need a minute, Nana." She pulled him into the bedroom and shut the door. Once alone, she whispered, "Okay, how much trouble am I really in?"

"You're in forty thousand worth."

She blinked several times as her mouth slowly lowered. "What the— What happened to the other sixty?"

"Take a guess."

"Lorraine."

"That's my thought."

Carrie slapped her hands and raised her voice. "Oh, that woman."

From the other room, Shirley Tilson called back, "What woman?"

Skeeter whispered, "The detective's theory is that the forty thousand in your purse came from Mason's safe."

Carrie's face whitened. "That's my motive for killing him? Why would I do that? Why would I steal from Mason?"

"You stole a hundred from the mob."

She smirked. "But they don't know that, and I already told you I regretted it."

"That'll play well during your defense. Now you need to explain how you have that much cash in your purse. Do writers usually carry that much around?"

"In their dreams." Carrie lowered her head.

"Can you come up with an excuse?"

"Maybe. I don't know. Oh, man, I should never have come here."

"You should never have stolen the money, either."

She rolled her eyes. "No kidding. Geez, you know how to kick a woman when she's down."

"What was going on between you and Mason?"

"You mean why did I hate him so much?"

Skeeter nodded.

"He accused me of stalking him at a writer's conference."

"Were you?"

"No." Her face pinched. "He's old enough to be my grandfather."

"Then why did he accuse you?"

"To divert attention from what he'd done. He'd stolen an idea for one of my stories, and I was mad about it."

Skeeter squinted. "If you hated him so much, how did he hear about the idea?"

She waved a hand. "I didn't always hate him. In fact, for a long time, I sort of looked up to him. How could I not? He was Mason friggin' Freemantle. The guy was a legend. A couple of years ago, at one of the conferences, we talked after an event. He said he knew my grandmother from the tower, and that was sort of an ice breaker. We hit it off after that. He had a reputation in the industry as a flirt, but I never saw it. Instead, he seemed interested in me as an author." She shook her head. "He kept mentioning Nana, so I thought he was sweet on her. He knew about my books and complimented my writing. Of course, I was flattered that Mason even knew who I was. He was such an experienced writer, and I'm barely known in the true-crime circles. So, when he asked what I was working on, I told him."

"What was your story about?"

Carrie crossed her arms. "It was supposed to be about a Kennebunkport con artist. I was going to title it *The Maine Squeeze*. Mason intently listened while I laid out the whole thing. When I finished, he wished me luck with it. I was on cloud nine after talking with him about it."

"So?"

"Then I read in the trades that his next project was about a female con artist called *The Portland Squeeze.*"

Skeeter remembered seeing the book in Otto's room.

"One of the Hollywood studios optioned the story before it was released." She gritted her teeth. "He stole my idea—the whole shebang—and reaped the rewards because of it."

Skeeter asked, "How many people knew about this?"

"A few, I guess. Why?"

"Because if the cops learn about this, they'll have another motive—revenge."

Carrie suddenly appeared wobbly, and Skeeter grabbed her by the arm.

For a moment, she took deep breaths to settle

herself. When the color returned to her cheeks, she nodded. "Sorry about that."

"It's okay. The cop downstairs told me Mason had some financial troubles after a divorce and a legal battle over plagiarism. Was that you?"

"I was never married to him." She dismissively waved her hand. "Bad joke. And no, I didn't accuse him of plagiarism. How could I? I'd barely started on that story by the time he banged his out."

"What happened with the plagiarism case?"

"He won. And just so you don't think the loser of the case could be the killer, that author died shortly after the verdict. Suicide."

Skeeter knew a homicide could be made to look like a suicide. However, that seemed like a lot of work for Mason Freemantle to do. And why would the man need to do it after he won the plagiarism case? More than likely, the author who lost simply felt depressed and decided to end it all.

"Who was the author? Was it anyone I might have heard of?"

Carrie shook her head. "I doubt it. I don't even remember his name. He was an unknown—just some weekend plinker that Mason met at a conference. The guy made the mistake of sharing his story. Sound familiar? Anyway, before the guy could find a publisher, Mason announced his book, an almost exact copy of this guy's idea. His suicide was a sad story. He left behind a wife and a young daughter. I think that's what always stuck with me about that story. The damage to the people on the periphery of the event."

Skeeter said, "It sounds like Mason had a history of stealing the ideas of others."

"That's how I feel. No one else believes it, though."

"What about his stalking accusation bothered you?"

"Besides the fact that it was false?"

Embarrassment washed over Skeeter's face. "Yeah. Sorry."

"Don't be. He said it so I would stop bothering him. What made the accusation worse was the conference leaders believed him. I'm not sure if you know this, but he could be very charming when he wanted to be."

"A charming grandfather is what you're saying."

She cast a sideways glance. "Right."

"Why wouldn't the directors believe you?"

"You think they should believe me because I'm a woman?"

Skeeter lifted an eyebrow. "Well..."

"It only goes that way in the high-profile cases—the ones that make news. I think they believed him for a couple reasons. Probably the most important is that he's a big name. Everyone knew Mason Freemantle."

"I didn't know him until I got here."

"People who *read* know him."

"Did you make a counter-accusation?"

Carrie shrugged. "I did, but he accused me of stalking first. Once that happened, anything I said sounded like sour grapes. A cloud of suspicion had already been cast over me."

"And you didn't have any proof to your story?"

Her head bounced from side to side. "I had my notes, but scribbles on random pieces of paper aren't a published story. And I never showed those to Mason. The truth was I didn't have a leg to stand on."

"But you were still angry."

"Wouldn't you be?" Her face reddened. "After the last conference, my publisher warned that I was on probation. My agent said pretty much the same thing. Maybe that's why I did the thing with the mob. I don't know. Hindsight isn't always twenty-twenty. Based on his reputation, I probably should have been suspicious that he wasn't simply nice. He was after something all right."

Skeeter shoved his hands into his pockets. He was running out of time which meant Carrie was as well.

He needed to take her somewhere safe that the cops couldn't intimidate their way into or easily request a search warrant. The cops would knock and politely ask for permission to search the apartment for a writer suspected of murder. Skeeter suspected most would agree to let them search. What he needed was an ally—someone who would willingly hide Carrie Fenton if the cops ever showed up at their door.

He asked, "How did you get here?"

"The stairs? How else? It's not rocket science." She pulled on the baggy drab-green uniform. "That's why I put on this. I didn't want anyone to notice me."

"The uniform calls more attention than distracts. You should probably change out of it."

She unbuttoned the shirt and shrugged the shirt from her shoulders. It had been slipped on over her sweater. Next, she shimmied out of the pants that she had worn over her jeans.

"Did you hear anyone in the stairwell when you came up?"

"There was someone above me that was coming down. I stayed close to the walls so they couldn't see me."

Skeeter said, "We need to move you."

"To where? You already said the cops are on every exit."

"I have an idea. Let's go."

***

They left Shirley Tilson in her apartment. She wasn't going to be able to ascend the fourteen floors necessary. As they climbed, neither talked. They needed to get out of the stairwell as quickly as possible. If a police officer found them in there, Carrie would be detained. Skeeter might even be held for aiding and abetting. He wasn't too worried about that, though. He was more concerned about being stuck in jail somewhere that friends of the Dawgs or the mob could get at him.

They had just passed the eighth floor when a door opened into the stairwell far below.

Multiple voices traveled upward before the footfalls started. Skeeter wanted to stop and look, to see if he could count how many were coming but doing so meant someone might be able to see him.

He leaned against the wall and whispered, "Hurry."

Carrie did so, but this caused her to trip on the next lunge upward. As she fell, her hands slapped the stair in front of her, and she expelled a large whoosh of air. Hoping not to slow their climb, Skeeter wrapped an arm around her waist and lifted her back to her feet. The two of them hurried as silently as they could.

"Is someone up there?" a voice hollered from below.

They continued up the next flight.

"Hello?" the voice hollered again. "Who's up there?"

Skeeter stopped Carrie at the tenth floor and held his finger to his lips. Below a voice said, "Hey, Metcalf, are you still up on seventeen?"

A radio squawked before Officer Metcalf replied, "*Yeah?*"

"Someone's in the east stairwell. Start down, will ya? Let's see who this is."

"*I'm on my way.*"

As quietly as he could, Skeeter opened the door to the tenth floor and pushed Carrie into the hallway.

From below, boots ran up the stairwell. Above Skeeter, a door clanged open.

"Whoever's down there," Officer Metcalf shouted, "if you know what's good for you, step out where we can see you."

Skeeter pulled the door closed behind him. Then he turned to Carrie, who watched him with evident fear. "Run!"

They sprinted along the corridor then turned into the west hallway. They ran the rest of the tenth floor. When they arrived at the opposite end, Skeeter leaned a shoulder into the door, and it popped open into that stairwell. Once Carrie was clear, Skeeter spun and pushed the door closed.

"Up," he said. "Don't stop until you get to the sixteenth."

The two of them rushed up the stairs as if their freedom depended on it.

Chapter 17

Floyd and Beatrice Ketterling stood side by side in their living room.

Mrs. Ketterling clutched a copy of *Maine Line Murder* to her chest. "It's a real honor to have you in our home."

Carrie Fenton was bent at the waist with her hands on her knees. She gasped as she struggled to steady her breathing. Lifting a hand, Carrie acknowledged Beatrice's compliment.

"Thanks for letting us in," Skeeter said.

Floyd smiled. "Of course. How could we not? We're big fans."

Skeeter moved to the window so he could see what was occurring down below. Several more patrol cars were in the parking lot now. He could make them out by the light bars on their roofs. The news vans parked on the sidewalk had multiplied. It was hard to make out the reporters in the crowd below, but it seemed that there were multiple cameras pointed at the building. Maybe it was his imagination.

Mr. Ketterling watched Skeeter as he returned to the others. "There are rumors—"

"Not that we believe them," Beatrice interjected.

Floyd chuckled. "No, of course not. We'd never believe them."

Carrie asked, "What rumors?"

Beatrice nervously danced from foot to foot. She clutched the book tighter to her chest. "That Mason Freemantle was murdered."

"It's true," Skeeter said.

Mrs. Ketterling stopped moving and covered her mouth with her book. From behind *Maine Line Murder*, she said, "Right above us? On the seventeenth?"

Skeeter nodded.

Floyd cleared his throat and leaned toward Carrie. "And there's also some speculation—"

She stiffened. "I didn't have anything to do with it."

"Well, no, my dear." Mr. Ketterling chuckled again, but this time it seemed forced and filled with nervous energy. "Of course not. You couldn't have anything to do with it."

"But the rumors," Beatrice said, "you know. Even the silly ones make a person stop and think."

"You're one of our favorite authors," Floyd added. "We couldn't imagine you doing such a thing."

Skeeter studied the Ketterlings. "You've been in your apartment all day. Did you hear what was going on, or has someone called?"

Beatrice shook her head.

Mr. Ketterling's gaze shifted to the TV. Skeeter walked over and put his hand on it. The box was warm.

"The news?"

"We saw all the activity from the window,"

Floyd said. "We wanted to know what was going on."

Mrs. Ketterling nodded. "It's weird to see the tower on TV. It's almost like one of those shows we hate, but it's better than them because it's real."

Floyd faced his wife. "But it's not better because it's where we live."

"Oh, yes," Beatrice said. "It's where we live. And it happened right above us."

Skeeter asked, "Why would you think it was only a rumor if the news reported it?"

Mr. Ketterling pushed his glasses up his nose. "Fake news. They could have made the whole thing up. Or twisted it to suit them."

Beatrice held up her book. "The only thing we trust is what we read."

"But not fiction," Floyd interjected.

"Oh my, no."

"Or the newspapers."

"Definitely not the newspapers." Beatrice beamed at Carrie. "Only writers like you tell the truth."

Carrie seemed embarrassed by the sudden praise of her trustworthiness. "Thank you."

Skeeter moved closer to Carrie. "What else did the news say?"

"Not much," Floyd said. "They said there was a suspect in the building." He motioned toward Carrie, "but we didn't believe them."

"Fake news," Carrie repeated.

Floyd winked at her. "It's like they're always trying to convince us of something."

"Selling us," Beatrice added.

"The news should be the news," Floyd said. "No flash. No sizzle. Just the facts."

"What did the news say?" Skeeter asked again.

Floyd glanced at the TV. "We watched a couple of channels. The reporters said essentially the same thing. The police had two persons of interest, but they didn't say who it was. When you two showed up at our door out of breath—"

Beatrice touched her husband's arm. "Don't forget sweaty. Especially him."

Floyd eyed Skeeter. "Out of breath and sweaty when the police are looking for a murder suspect are two things that don't lend themselves to credibility."

The older couple had a point, so Skeeter said the only thing he could think of in that moment. "Fake news."

"Exactly," Beatrice said. She held up *Maine Line Murder.* "That's why books are important." She smiled brightly. "They tell the truth. You couldn't have done it. Could you?"

"I promise," Carrie said. "Cross my heart."

Beatrice clutched her book tightly to her, and then she glanced to Skeeter. "What about him?" she whispered.

"He didn't do it either."

Floyd put his hand on Skeeter's shoulder and squeezed. "I knew it. This one's a good man. He doesn't seem capable of hurting anyone."

Carrie raised an eyebrow.

"Can she stay here?" Skeeter asked.

"Oh, yes," Beatrice blurted. Her book bowed due to the tight grip. "I mean, most assuredly. We would like that."

"If the police show up—"

Floyd lifted a hand to stop him. "You let me handle them. They have no business coming into our home. We won't be pushed around."

Beatrice smiled. "Floyd can be adamant when he wants to be. There was a pushy meter reader once who got an earful about just walking onto our property."

"He never did that again," Mr. Ketterling said with pride.

Skeeter nodded his thanks to the older couple and headed for the door. Carrie followed along.

She asked, "Where are you going?"

"Now that you're safe, I'm still going to try and clear your name, but I'm running out of time."

"Because of the cops? The search and all?"

"Something like that." He didn't want to tell her about Marshal Goodspeed sitting outside in her car.

He put his hand on the knob. To stop him from opening the door, she covered his hand with hers.

"Why are you helping me?" she asked.

"It's the right thing to do."

Carrie cocked her head. "You could just leave and get a new name."

"That's still going to happen, but right now, you need a friend who believes in you. I've been in that situation. Let me help."

She removed her hand, and he opened the door. Skeeter stepped into the hallway.

***

He checked the east stairwell. There were no cops in it now. Had there been, he would have acted accordingly and gone up to talk with Detective Reddy. Instead, he descended the stairs, taking two at a time, until he stepped into the first-floor hallway.

Across the way, the kitchen bustled with activity. Members of the staff hurriedly returned to preparing the meal that was interrupted earlier. The head chef, Angel, noticed him and approached. "Hello, my friend." His eyes narrowed. "You are all sweaty. What have you been doing?"

"Running to the top of the world."

Now, the chef questioningly eyed him. "And what did you see?"

"A lid blocking my path."

Angel's brow furrowed. "A riddle." He touched his chin. "I am not sure what to make of that."

Skeeter looked toward the lobby. The noise was still there, but it seemed less hostile now. There might even have been a tone of joy in it.

"What's going on?" the big man asked.

Angel thumbed toward the commotion. "The cop told us to go back to work. Eh, it is better than standing around. Am I right? More cops have arrived as are others with cameras and toolboxes."

The crime scene technicians, thought Skeeter. He glanced down the hallway again.

"Can I get you anything?" Angel asked.

"Have you seen Charlotte?"

"She's talking with the fat policeman."

"And Lorraine?"

The chef smirked. "She is outside with the press. She seems to be enjoying her moment in the spotlight. I need to get back to work. We are behind."

"Angel, let me ask you a question. Do you know anywhere that Lorraine could put something small—" Skeeter mimed a little box with his hands "—that only a few people would know of?"

The chef seemed to think about it for a moment, then shook his head. "No. I am sorry. I do not know of this place."

Skeeter thanked his new friend then left.

He stopped at the edge of the lobby to survey the activity. The crowd had thinned slightly. Some folks headed into the dining facility. Others proceeded down the west hall toward the dayroom. Likely, it was to sit rather than to stand.

A few headed by him for the nearest stairwell. This included the ladies in the tracksuits and the man in the headband. He didn't seem happy as he brought up the rear.

"If we take the stairs," he whined, "I swear to heaven I'm going to pass out. My blood sugar—"

The women collectively groaned as they

hurried into the stairwell.

"Wait for me," the man griped. "I'm so dehydrated."

Across the lobby, Charlotte stood with both Officers Baggiano and Metcalf. Several other officers waited nearby. They wore the expressions of most waiting cops—a mixture of boredom and vigilance. Their alert eyes were juxtaposed against slack faces and relaxed postures.

A group of younger folks in plain clothes waited behind the cops. By their bright eyes and lack of weapons, Skeeter surmised that they were the crime scene technicians. They had several toolkits with them—a large plastic one, a square briefcase, and two red ones resembling elaborate fishing kits.

His gaze drifted outside.

Lorraine Bagley stood in front of several reporters and camera operators. She wildly gesticulated as she spoke. Skeeter wondered what had her so animated.

"Where the heck have you been, son?" Clancy poked him in the arm to get his attention. Muriel and Edna flanked him.

"Things are a little crazy right now."

Muriel stepped forward. "We want to see the blue cat."

"I told you—"

"His name is Blue," Clancy said, "yeah, yeah. Doesn't matter. I don't believe you. I think you're fibbin' just like Charlotte."

"About the name?"

"We want to see him," Edna interjected.

Muriel leaned forward. "You said we could."

Skeeter eyed the three. "Why's it so important?"

"This old dodger," Muriel thumbed toward Clancy, "bet us that you don't have a cat."

"But I do," Skeeter said. "I told you."

Muriel smirked at the older man. "Told you so."

"That don't prove nothing," Clancy said confidently. "I could say I walked on the moon, and you don't know if I did or didn't." He impatiently tapped his four-legged cane on the ground. "Until then, it's your word against mine."

"Yeah," Edna said to Skeeter. "We need to prove it."

The big man shook his head. He didn't have time for this type of delay. "What's this bet you made?"

Muriel said, "If you don't have a cat—"

"Which he doesn't," Clancy said.

"—then we have to sit with him at the next movie night."

"And if I do have a cat?"

Edna said, "Then Clancy has to make a quilt with us."

The older man exaggeratedly rolled his eyes and put a hand over his heart. "Heaven take me now."

Muriel nodded. "It'll serve you right."

Skeeter asked, "Who came up with this bet?"

Both women pointed to Clancy, who looked

pleased with himself.

"So, you ladies go to the movies with him if he wins, and if he loses, he's forced to make a quilt with you?"

Muriel and Edna nodded. "That's right."

Skeeter smiled at the older man. "My room is down the hall, Brer Rabbit. It's open. Feel free to go look at the cat."

Clancy winked at Skeeter, then turned to the ladies. "All right, you two. I'm gonna prove you wrong and get my movie night." He hobbled down the east hall.

Edna whispered, "Did he call Clancy, Bear Abbot? What's that about?"

"I thought he said, Bad Habit." Muriel shrugged. "Doesn't matter. Let's prove that old dodger wrong and win that bet."

The two ladies hurried after Clancy.

"Skeeter!" Charlotte called.

He faced her and the group of officers that studied him expectantly.

It was never a good thing when that many cops watched anything. A group of officers watching an intersection meant people were getting tickets. A group of lawmen watching a house suggested it was getting raided. A group of cops watching a sporting event meant they weren't doing their job. To Skeeter, the latter was the least offensive of the bunch.

But now, there were seven cops and five crime scene technicians watching him—he'd hesitated long enough to count them all. One of the officers held an unlaced boot—it appeared to be highly polished.

"What's with the boot?" Skeeter asked.

Baggiano motioned toward the officer holding it. "He found it in the parking lot. We think it belongs to the maintenance man everyone is looking for."

Skeeter imagined Otto on the roof, trying to signal people below. He probably took off the boot and tossed it over the side.

"Our theory," Baggiano said, "is your boss ran from the building and left it behind."

"So, you figure Otto Cantrell ran so fast that he literally came out of a boot and now is clomping around Chicago with one bare foot?"

Baggiano glared at him. "I didn't say it was a good theory."

"What's Detective Reddy say about it?"

"We haven't told her yet."

With her head, Charlotte motioned toward Chicago's finest. "They want to know if you've had any luck with the elevators."

"Yeah, Dursky," Officer Baggiano said. Irritation laced his voice. "When are you going to turn those things on?"

Metcalf nodded. "Don't make me walk those stairs back up to Reddy again. She wants you to get those things running."

Skeeter didn't like everyone's eyes on him, and anger brewed in his gut. His time was running out to prove Carrie Fenton was innocent, and this elevator issue was only slowing him down.

Besides, Charlotte already knew everything

Skeeter did about the elevators. Only Otto and Lorraine had a key to start or stop them. And the building's manager claimed someone had taken hers. As far as anyone else knew, Otto was still missing. Only Skeeter and Mason's killer knew where Otto was.

If the assistant manager was playing dumb with the cops, he wanted to know why. "You know everything I do about the elevators, Charlotte. Why not tell them?"

Her eyes widened, and she glanced toward the assembled members of the law enforcement community. Both Baggiano and Metcalf seemed surprised at Skeeter's terse response.

Nervously, Charlotte chuckled. Then she reached out and rubbed the big man's arm. Her hand lingered on his bicep. "Skeeter's under a lot of pressure today. What with everything going on." She faced him now, and her eyes narrowed. "Who would you call at a time like this?"

"The elevator company, but I don't know which one."

She nodded knowingly. "Oh, sure. It's only your third day. Well, if you don't know who to call and I don't know—which I already told these nice fellas, by the way—who would know?"

Skeeter slowly said, "Lorraine." Then he glanced out the window. "She was going to call the elevator company and get someone out here."

Charlotte's face relaxed. "Right. Lorraine was supposed to call the elevator company."

Skeeter studied her. "You know she was. You were there when she said it."

The assistant manager turned to Officer Baggiano. "I wonder why she didn't call them?"

"Maybe she did," Skeeter said, but no one heard him.

Baggiano and Metcalf were already on their way to the door with the rest of the cops in their wake.

Charlotte patted his arm a couple of times. "You did great, Skeeter. Really great. Thank you." She hurried after the cops into the parking lot.

Skeeter stood in the lobby and wondered what game Charlotte was playing. He glanced at the clock on the wall. His time was running short. He had to make decisions quickly, or he'd be forced to leave the tower.

He quickly inventoried the players in Mason Freemantle's death.

Otto was locked on the roof.

Lorraine and Charlotte were now in the parking lot with the cops.

Carrie Fenton was hiding with the Ketterlings on the sixteenth floor.

Detective Kajal Reddy was on the seventeenth with the body of Mason Freemantle.

But Skeeter was still missing something. He wanted to talk with someone to bounce ideas off. He'd done that before with his previous witness inspector and his FBI handler. Why couldn't he do that with the U.S. Marshal now waiting outside?

He walked down the east hallway. He wasn't sure that Gayle Goodspeed had talked to the cop guarding this door, but it made the most sense. Had she come in the other way, she would have had to pass through the lobby—too many people would have seen her.

As he passed his room, he heard Muriel and Edna exclaim, "We won! There is a cat!"

He could only imagine Clancy's excitement at being 'forced' to quilt with the ladies. Brer Rabbit had just been thrown into the briar patch.

Skeeter pushed open the door and stepped outside. The cop standing there said, "I'm sorry, sir. No one's allowed to leave the building at this time."

"I need to speak to the woman over there." For additional clarity, Skeeter pointed to where Gayle Goodspeed sat in the Chevy Impala. A waft of cigarette smoke trailed up from the driver's side window.

The officer's gaze followed the direction of Skeeter's finger. When the cop understood what was being asked, he nodded. "Yes, sir," he said and looked away.

Skeeter trotted across the parking lot, opened the passenger door, and settled into the car.

Goodspeed eyed him. "Ready to go?"

"Not yet," the big man said. "I need some help."

Chapter 18

"And that's where I'm at," Skeeter said. He'd just spent the last several minutes relaying everything he'd learned. He couldn't tell how much time had passed since he began, but he judged it by how much Goodspeed had smoked. She finished two cigarettes and was about to light a third.

She held the lighter at the end of her next. "And what do you want from me?"

"I wanted to see what you thought. Maybe get a professional opinion."

"Do you think we're buddies?"

"No."

Goodspeed lit the cigarette then expelled a line of smoke. "So, we're peers?"

"Definitely not."

With the two fingers that held the cigarette, she tapped the in-dash clock. "You're running out of time, Beau. Thirty minutes left."

"Help me then."

"I am helping you—by getting you someplace safe."

"But this matters."

The marshal shook her head. "It doesn't."

"To me, it does."

Even though there was no ash at the end of her cigarette, she knocked it out the window. "Your safety matters to me, and it matters to the

U.S. government, which trumps us both."

"I want to figure this out."

"What you want is irrelevant."

Skeeter hated that sentiment. He'd spent his whole life as an outlaw. He did what he wanted, where he wanted, when he wanted. No one could tell him no. Sometimes that put him on the wrong side of the law, but it always made his desires relevant.

Sternly, he said, "Carrie Fenton and Otto Cantrell didn't kill Mason Freemantle."

The marshal observed him for a moment then shook her head. "This is not a smart move, Beau." She put her fingers on the key stuck in the ignition. "I have a good mind to start this thing and drive away."

"Not without my cat."

She smirked. "You left him behind once before."

"I had no choice. We have a choice now."

"Travis is a good boy." Her fingers slipped from the key. "Unlike you."

"The story of my life. So, before I go back in there, help me see what I'm missing."

"Why should I? You're the one who wants to play amateur sleuth."

"I'm not playing anything."

She inhaled deeply on her cigarette. When she spoke, entrails of smoke floated from her mouth. "Sometimes, the simplest answer is the right one."

"What's that supposed to mean?"

"The woman did it."

"Carrie? By herself? No way. She's innocent."

"How do you know?"

"I just know is how I know."

"Oh, well, if you know." Goodspeed rolled her eyes. "How do you think that would work if you were arrested? I'll tell you. It wouldn't. You're sitting in witness protection talking with a marshal for a reason—the facts. Stick to them. You already told me that this Fenton woman had the most motive to kill Mason Freemantle. Believe it and move on."

Skeeter looked away. "She didn't do it."

"Because you know."

He didn't respond.

"Fine. Otto did it. He was jealous of the attention Mason Freemantle was getting from Shirley what's-her-name. Whack, boom, over the head, one less writer in this world."

"But Otto was stuck on the roof."

"A minor detail."

Skeeter eyed her.

Goodspeed shrugged. "I'll give you that one. If he was locked on the roof, it's problematic." She inhaled on the cigarette. "Go with the manager then. She might have had a secret relationship. Although, you haven't proved that, right?"

"No, but she stole the money."

"She did? Have you found the proof of that? I didn't think so. There's a lot of things you don't know about the manager."

Skeeter leaned in. "Is she your other witness?"

The marshal smirked. "You wish."

He flopped back into his seat. "Well, Lorraine hasn't been upset by Mason's death."

Goodspeed waved her cigarette as she spoke. "So what? Maybe there wasn't a secret relationship. Did you ever really see anything between them, beyond flirting?"

Skeeter hadn't.

"There you go," the marshal said, "right back to the Fenton woman. She did it. Let the locals handle it. Grab your cat, and let's skedaddle."

"Carrie didn't do it."

"So, it's Charlotte, then. Get Travis. Maybe we can grab a burger at White Castle on the way out of town."

He eyed the marshal. "And if she did?"

"What would I care? We're burning daylight with all this supposing."

"*She's* not the other one in witness protection?"

Goodspeed shook her head. "Good Lord, Beau. How would you figure that?"

"It seemed she was looking for Carrie. And I think she's pushing the cops toward Lorraine."

"That's what you've based your decision on? Her searching for a missing suspect and her suggesting the manager might be involved, too? Maybe the gal is bucking for a promotion. Ever think of that?"

He stared at her.

"Or maybe she was doing it out of concern for society. Or maybe," the marshal leaned toward him, "she was doing it because she's sweet on you."

"How would you know that?"

"She is, isn't she?"

"I don't know. Maybe. But how did you know?"

"Simple deduction."

Skeeter snapped his fingers. "The other witness told you. Or she did, and you're trying to throw me off the trail."

"It's not her, Beau."

"Who then?"

"I made the whole thing up."

Skeeter turned in his seat to face her. "C'mon, Goodspeed. What's it going to hurt to tell me?" Skeeter eyed the clock. "I'm out of here in twenty-seven minutes."

The marshal leaned back against the headrest and took another drag from her cigarette. She blew the cigarette smoke out of the window. "If you want a story, I'll give you one."

"Stop messing with me and just tell me."

"He went into the program as a young man— barely old enough to drink at a bar."

Skeeter groaned.

"If you don't want the story, that's fine by me."

It was his turn to point at the in-dash clock. "But my time."

"I know. It's getting low. But as I was saying, he was barely old enough to drink at a bar. He was known as Earl Pritie."

"Pretty? Like in cute?"

"No." She spelled the last name then. "But

Earl was a handsome kid, and he knew it." She said it almost wistfully before inhaling on the cigarette again. "It was a shame what the government did to him."

Skeeter eyed her waiting for the marshal to continue, but Goodspeed didn't speak. Instead, she stared off into the distance. The big man tapped the in-dash clock. "I've got to go."

She tossed the cigarette out of the window then put both hands on the steering wheel. "Earl Pritie was a Soviet citizen."

Skeeter shifted in his seat. "A spy?"

"Yeah. No." Goodspeed seemed irritated. "Well, sort of."

"Which is it?"

"His parents were spies. They were trained by the Soviets and sent over during the height of the cold war. They lived like Americans, got jobs, and waited for the occasional assignment."

"Can that even happen?"

She laughed. "Boy, are you out of the loop. Of course, it can happen. We called it the Illegals Program. The Soviets had another name, of course. Something dreadfully Russian and depressing. Anyway, the Soviets drafted intelligent teenagers and taught them how to act and talk like Americans."

To Skeeter, it sounded like an implausible movie.

Goodspeed continued and she seemed to have a head of steam with her retelling now. "There was even an American village in Russia that these young spies lived in. They spoke

English, watched American television, and ate American food. The Soviets cut those kids off from all contact with their families. There was no going back. Burn the boats, so to speak."

Skeeter thought the marshal might be shining him on now. The whole idea seemed too fantastical.

"When the boy's parents reached an age and level of sophistication, the Soviets put them in Boston."

"Why Boston?"

She shrugged. "Why not? They plunked their sleeper agents down throughout the country in places where they could get easy access to flights and where they could blend into the background. Whenever the Soviets needed them, they'd drive or catch a flight."

"And what did Earl Pritie do?"

"He didn't do anything. Weren't you listening? He was a kid. Born in America and raised on comic books, Pepsi commercials, and Chuck Norris movies. When he found out his parents were communists, he contacted us."

"The marshals?"

Goodspeed smirked. "No, Beau, he contacted the government. Regardless of his parents, he was an all-American boy. He loved Ronald Reagan and wanted to fight for truth, justice, and the American way."

"That's Superman."

"Like I said, he liked comics."

"And why is he hiding in the program?"

"Because we caught his parents. We picked

up some chatter that the Soviets wanted Earl. Maybe to trade for the parents. Maybe so he couldn't reveal anything he might have seen or learned."

Skeeter thought about the men he'd met in the building. Comic books and Pepsi had been around for years, but the Chuck Norris comment bothered him. Even though he didn't watch a lot of movies, he knew who Chuck Norris was. He'd watched some of his films as a kid. And he was confident the guy wasn't acting before the seventies. Which meant most of the guys living in the building were already adults by that time.

He eyed the marshal. "The other witness can't be a resident in the building and have grown up on Chuck Norris movies. It doesn't make sense."

"Did I ever say the other witness was a resident in the building?" Goodspeed cocked her head. "I'm pretty sure I never said that. I think I said—"

"He was in the building." Skeeter nodded. "He's on the kitchen staff. Isn't he?"

Goodspeed remained silent but smiled now. "It's a pretty good story, huh?"

Skeeter thought about the staff then. Angel was the oldest in the group, and he was only a few years older than Skeeter. And everyone working there was of an ethnic group that seemed different than Eastern Europe.

So, if the other witness wasn't a resident of the tower and he wasn't a kitchen staff member, who else could it be? Skeeter's gaze drifted to the uniformed man guarding the exit door.

"He's a cop."

Goodspeed grunted noncommittally.

Skeeter felt a spike of adrenaline. He was on the right track.

When Marshal Goodspeed told Skeeter another witness was inside the building, there were only three cops inside the building. Detective Kajal Reddy was a woman, so that removed her from the equation. That left the very young Metcalf and—

"Baggiano," Skeeter said. "Earl Pritie is Baggiano."

"Did I say that?"

"You didn't have to."

"I could be making this all up."

"Why would you do that?"

"Because I like messing with you, Little Sister. It pleases me in a way I can't explain."

"You wouldn't do that."

"Whatever you say."

"Are you going to move Baggiano now?"

"I don't know who you're talking about." She removed a new cigarette from a pack.

"But I know who he is."

"Good luck with that." Goodspeed tapped the clock. "You've got twenty-two minutes, Beau. I hope this has been helpful."

Skeeter opened the car door but paused. "Why are you letting me do this?"

She raised an eyebrow.

"Your predecessor would have dragged me out of here, kicking and screaming if he had to.

He wouldn't have let me go back inside."

Goodspeed studied her unlit cigarette. "Contrary to what I said, Beau, what you want isn't irrelevant. Some men willingly bend to the program, and they do just fine. Those who struggle with it need a little room to figure out who they are. To find out if the program can benefit them in the long run."

Skeeter slipped entirely from the car now.

"The next time you come out," the marshal said. "Bring your cat."

Chapter 19

As Skeeter hurried back to the building, the cop guarding the east hallway pulled open the door.

"Good luck," the officer said.

He paused for a moment. Maybe the cop guarding the door was the other in the program. Perhaps that was how Goodspeed had gotten in. But hadn't the marshal said the other witness was inside the building?

Skeeter was now messing with his own mind, and he needed to focus on helping Carrie Fenton.

He passed by his room then the kitchen. Angel waved, but the big man was on a mission. He had twenty minutes to wrap everything up and get back outside to Marshal Goodspeed.

When he stepped into the lobby, a group of residents surrounded Clancy, Muriel, and Edna. The two women were gleefully retelling the story of how they won the bet about Skeeter's cat. Clancy tried to appear disappointed by the idea of quilting with the two women, but a sly grin hovered at the corner of his mouth.

Outside in the parking lot, Lorraine Bagley was surrounded by several officers. It appeared as if two cops intensely interviewed her. Charlotte stood by and watched with a satisfied smirk.

Behind them was a line of reporters and camera operators.

And now, a small throng of Mason Freemantle fans had gathered. Some carried homemade signs professing their love, devotion, and willingness to marry him beyond the grave. Others brought unlit candles—perhaps hoping this would go into the evening and morph into a vigil of some sort.

Standing in the corner of the lobby near the entry to the dining hall was Officer Baggiano, Officer Metcalf, and the officer with the boot.

Upon seeing Skeeter, Baggiano loudly said, "This guy," and motioned him over. "Are you ever going to get the elevators working?"

He said, "I'm working on it," even though he wasn't. He was doing a lot of lying again. He didn't want to do it but living in witness protection didn't seem the easiest way to practice honesty.

The officer next to Baggiano held up the boot. "We got a new theory on this."

Skeeter didn't want to delay further with the cops, but if they had a theory on Otto's disappearance, he wanted to hear it—even if it took a minute. He didn't need the maintenance supervisor's sudden appearance to throw everything off. "What's the theory?"

Officer Baggiano moved the gum around in his mouth before speaking. "The white shirts seem to think your boss might have been kidnapped, and his boot fell off in the process."

The other officers murmured their dissatisfaction with the administration's theory.

Skeeter asked, "What has Detective Reddy said about it?"

Metcalf pointed to the elevators. "We'll tell her when the elevators are fixed."

"Or when he hauls himself up those stairs," Baggiano said to the younger cop with the boot.

"Why me?"

"Because you're the one holding the boot."

Skeeter motioned Baggiano to step aside.

"What?" the portly cop said. He smacked his gum a couple of times. "You got a secret or something?"

"I want to talk with you—alone."

Baggiano frowned and glanced toward the other cops. They watched him with obvious suspicion.

"It's important," Skeeter said.

"Okay," Baggiano muttered, drawing the word out into two long syllables. He reluctantly stepped aside with the big man.

When they were out of earshot, Skeeter said, "I know."

"You know what?"

"About you."

Baggiano smirked. "I don't know what you're implying, pal."

"Marshal Goodspeed told me."

"I don't know anybody named Marshal Goodspeed. Is he one of the residents here?"

When faced with the truth of his past, Baggiano had to play obtuse—that was a word

Skeeter had recently learned and sort of liked. The cop couldn't openly admit who he was and where he came from. Denial must be deeply ingrained into his belief system.

Skeeter lowered his voice. "I know about your parents."

Baggiano stopped chewing his gum. "What about my parents?"

"About them being Soviets."

The cop leaned in and studied Skeeter's eyes. "Are you okay?"

"I'm fine."

"Have you been using any illegal narcotics?" Baggiano waggled his finger in front of Skeeter's eyes.

"You don't have to pretend with me. We're on the same side."

The officer returned to smacking on his gum. "What the heck are you talking about?"

"It's okay," Skeeter whispered. "I know your parents were spies. I won't tell."

Baggiano stiffened, and his eyes widened. "Spies? Are you serious?" Then he kicked his head back, and he guffawed.

Skeeter hadn't expected that reaction.

The overweight cop turned to the other officers. "This guy thinks my parents were spies!" Baggiano's voice resonated through the opened lobby.

The other officers burst into laughter and quickly crowded around Baggiano. Many of the residents turned to see what the commotion was about. Clancy, Muriel, and Edna led the crowd toward Skeeter.

Baggiano continued. "What makes you think my parents were Russian? No, wait. What did you say they were? You said they were Soviets." The cop touched his chest with both hands. "That means I'm a Soviet, too?" He clicked his heels together then sharply saluted Skeeter. "Dostoevsky, Comrade. Let me see your papers."

Skeeter wanted to walk away and pretend this moment never happened.

Baggiano stopped laughing. "Wait. If my parents were spies, does that mean I'm one, too? Like James Bond?"

Officer Metcalf muttered, "I think you have to be in shape to be a spy."

Baggiano smacked the younger cop's arm. "Watch it." The rotund officer tried to tuck the bottom of his shirt into his pants. "I'm in shape. What are you talking about?"

Metcalf moved closer to Skeeter. "Hey, wasn't there a TV show about Russian spies living in America?"

The cop with the boot said, "There was. I think this guy is making the whole thing up."

Marshal Goodspeed's words echoed in Skeeter's head—*I made the whole thing up.*

Baggiano stopped shoving his shirt back into place—one side billowed out while the other was now twisted. "You said we're on the same side. Are you a spy, too?"

Skeeter stiffened. "Me? No. I'm the assistant maintenance man."

"That's what you've said, but I don't see

anything being maintained. Do you guys?"

The cops and the crowd of residents all shook their heads.

Skeeter still wanted to pretend this moment never happened, but instead of walking away, he wanted to punch Baggiano.

The cop's brow furrowed. "What happened to my gum?" He anxiously patted his pockets. "Crud. I swallowed it." He looked to Skeeter. "Is this what you've been doing instead of fixing the elevator? Making up stories about my parents?"

The big man glanced around at the faces watching him. Clancy, Muriel, and Edna seemed to take extra interest in him.

Baggiano thumbed toward the cops standing behind him. "Are you going to make up stories about their parents, too?"

The cop with the boot said, "You better not."

Metcalf shrugged. "Doesn't bother me none unless you make them Packers fans. Then you'd have gone too far."

"Go Bears," Clancy muttered.

"Da Bears," Metcalf and the cop with the boot said in unison.

Skeeter wanted to say more to defend himself, but keeping his mouth shut seemed the best course of action in a situation like this.

Metcalf leaned in. "Where would you get such a crazy idea?"

Clancy lifted his four-legged cane and shook it so the bottom waggled. "It was probably that dadburn Charlotte. I saw the two of them skulking about. She was probably filling his melon with stories."

Baggiano shook his head. "You mean the assistant manager? No way. She's super helpful." He looked outside. "She told us how the manager was staying off her radio and that she didn't call the elevator company. We proved that to be true."

Outside, Lorraine appeared to be extremely nervous as the two cops continued their questioning. Charlotte happily nodded in response to whatever Lorraine was denying.

"See?" Baggiano said. "That woman is aces."

Muriel said, "She's always been nice."

"I think so, too," Edna offered. "She's a treasure."

"A real treasure," Muriel agreed.

Clancy's cane settled back to the floor, and he leaned his weight on it. "If you say so. I don't see it that way."

Muriel said, "You're a miserable old codger. You don't like anyone."

Edna's face scrunched. "Yeah. What she said."

Skeeter faced the older man. "Clancy, why do you believe Charlotte's not honest?"

"Because Otto told me she threw away a bunch of Mason Freemantle books, and he rescued them from the trash. When I asked her why she did such a thing, she denied it. She said she never read one of his books. So, who's fibbin? Her or Otto?"

Skeeter thought back to the books in Otto's room. When he saw them, he felt the handwriting in them was too feminine. He hadn't seen Otto's writing to compare it, though. If the books did indeed belong to Charlotte originally, that led to two questions. First, why did Charlotte throw them away in the first place? And second, why did Otto dig the books out of the trash?

The maintenance supervisor would later deny ever reading Mason Freemantle's work. Maybe he did that out of pride since Shirley Tilson seemed to fawn over the author. Was there another reason?

But Charlotte also denied ever reading Mason's work. Why would she need to deny it?

It was then that Skeeter realized there was a room he hadn't searched.

"I've got to go," he said.

Baggiano frowned and crossed his arms over his belly. "Where do you think you're going, Mr. Storyteller?"

"Yeah," Metcalf added.

Skeeter glanced around. "I've got to get the elevators started."

The portly cop smirked. "I thought you didn't know how."

"I think I know a way."

"Isn't that convenient?" Baggiano looked at Metcalf now. "I'm gonna go with this guy. You stay here with the boot."

The third cop held up the single piece of footwear. "I got a name, you know."

Skeeter said, "You don't need to go with me. I can handle it on my own."

Baggiano scoffed. "I'm gonna make sure you get those elevators started." He grabbed the big man by the arm. "Let's go, Shakespeare. Lead the way."

***

The two men stood outside Charlotte's apartment. Across the hallway was Otto's. Down the way was Lorraine Bagley's office.

"Is this your place?" Baggiano asked.

Skeeter grabbed the door handle. It was locked.

The cop chuckled. "Forget your key?"

Skeeter frowned. There were only two other rooms he'd found locked in the building. The manager's office, the salon, and now Charlotte's. He understood the reasoning behind the first two, but in a building where it was customary to leave one's apartment unlocked, why was Charlotte's secured?

He turned and hurried to the manager's office. Baggiano fell in behind him. "Where are you headed?"

Skeeter held his breath when he tried the handle to Lorraine's office. The door opened. She hadn't locked it after she returned. He didn't know if she always did or only occasionally. Perhaps she was distracted by the arrival of the press. Maybe she was preoccupied with hiding the money he suspected she stole from Carrie.

At the desk, he pulled open the middle drawer

and found the little keyring labeled Master.

"Are you gonna tell me what you're doing?" Baggiano asked.

"Trust me."

Skeeter ran by the cop. He didn't know how much time he had left before Marshal Goodspeed would insist he leave, but it couldn't be much. After slipping the key into Charlotte's door, he stepped into her apartment.

There was a scent of lavender—or what he suspected was an aroma of lavender. Regardless, it smelled nice, and it definitely smelled like a woman's apartment. There were pictures of cats on the wall. There were also photographs of a little girl and her father scattered about the room.

"This doesn't look like your room," Baggiano said. He moved toward one of the pictures. "Unless you were once a little girl."

There was a bookshelf in the room full of novels. There wasn't a single Mason Freemantle book in there. Skeeter grabbed one about a mystery-solving cat and flipped it open. In it, Charlotte had highlighted several passages and made multiple notes. He couldn't be sure, but Skeeter believed the handwriting to be the same. At the end of the book was a simple word, *Sweet*.

Baggiano slowly turned around as if reconsidering the apartment. "I think we're committing a burglary here, and by we, I mean you."

There weren't many places to hide things in

the small room. Skeeter tossed the book onto the bed and dropped to his knees. Underneath the bed was a small container. He slid it out and opened it. Inside were three items—a manila folder, a typed manuscript, and a key on a yellow tag.

The big man lifted the key from the box. "Here's Lorraine's missing elevator key." He slipped it into his pocket.

Baggiano said disappointedly, "It's always the nice ones that let you down."

Skeeter didn't believe that. In his experience, the nice ones tended to be nice. It was the awful people who consistently did terrible things, although, his perspective might have been skewed due to the people he lived around for many years. In retrospect, most of them were awful. Maybe living around nice people meant the occasional good one would let you down.

He next handed the stack of pages to Baggiano.

The cop flipped through it. "Is this what I think it is?"

"Looks to be that way."

Skeeter flipped open the folder. Inside were yellowed newspaper articles about the plagiarism lawsuit against Mason Freemantle. Skeeter didn't have time to read each article, but he found two pieces of information he needed.

The first was the plaintiff's name—Arthur Thrasher. The article explained he was an unpublished author from Albuquerque, New Mexico. In his obituary, it stated that Arthur was survived by his wife and daughter who were listed.

Skeeter stood and pointed at the obituary. "I think we've solved Mason Freemantle's murder."

"By committing a felony," Baggiano smirked. "We can't do this."

The big man waved the article. "But this gives us everything we need."

Baggiano carefully put the manuscript back into the box. "How are we going to prove it?" Then he gently took the obituary from Skeeter, tucked it into the manila folder, and put it back where it came from. "This was an illegal search, Skeeter. We can't use anything from here. Put the key back, too."

"But we know who did it."

"The courts will call it fruit of the poisonous tree. We can't obtain the evidence this way."

Skeeter wanted to throw his hands in the air and holler. Cops. Why did they always have to make things so complicated? He removed the key from his pocket and tossed it back into the container.

"Now, put the box under the bed. Where it belongs."

"If you want it under there, you do it."

Baggiano leaned an elbow on his gun. The sloppy gunfighter had returned. "We committed a felony. I'll arrest you right now for it and—"

"Whatever," Skeeter said. He didn't have time for the cop's holier-than-him stance. He grabbed the box, dropped it to the floor, and pushed it under the bed with his foot.

Baggiano snatched the big man by the arm and shoved him toward the door. "Let's get out of here before you get us both in trouble. I've worked too long to have my career go down the tubes following the likes of you. I'm starting to get the feeling that trouble follows you around like a lost puppy." Baggiano locked Charlotte's door and pulled it closed.

"What are we going to do now?"

The cop rubbed his face. "We know the proof exists, and it's in there."

"But what if she destroys it?"

"We better figure out a fast and legal way to get to it then."

"Can't you just say you had an unnamed source and go get it?"

Baggiano rolled his eyes. "That's not how it works."

"It's how it works on TV."

"Yeah? Well, guess what? This ain't TV."

Skeeter looked toward the lobby. "What if Charlotte confesses?"

"If she does that, the whole thing would work."

"Then I've got a plan."

"You?"

Skeeter nodded. "Can you bring Lorraine and Charlotte into the lobby?"

"Why am I doing the dirty work?"

"Because I've got to go to the basement to get something. It'll help us find Otto Cantrell."

"The missing maintenance man?"

Skeeter headed toward the stairwell door. "I think he's going to break this thing wide open."

"I thought we just did that."

Chapter 20

The assembled crowd in the lobby watched Skeeter and Officer Baggiano as they stood with Lorraine Bagley and Charlotte Olsen. Their voices raised with anticipation at the sight of new activity.

Angel and the kitchen staff now walked through the mass of people with trays of prepared snacks—sandwiches, veggies, and fruit cups. The residents happily took them and noshed while observing the law enforcement proceedings. Some residents had gone into the dining hall, but most remained to observe what was about to happen.

Huddled behind the building's manager were several police officers, including the one with the boot.

Lorraine huffed, then turned to Baggiano. "This is unacceptable. I've done nothing wrong."

"Relax," the portly cop said. "The detective is on the way. It'll all be over soon."

"But I've got things to do."

"Like call the elevator company?" Charlotte said.

Lorraine's face pickled. "I knew you were after my job."

The assistant manager shrugged. "It's not my fault you didn't call. Besides, it seems suspicious that you wouldn't do your job. Don't you agree, Officer?"

Charlotte looked expectantly to Baggiano, who only shrugged noncommittally. She frowned at his response then glanced at the other waiting officers. They seemed more receptive to her question, and several of them nodded their support. The cop with the boot raised it in sort of a toast.

The assistant manager then eyed Skeeter. "You agree, right? She never called the elevator company. It's totally suspicious that she didn't want them started."

He said, "I don't know."

"You don't know?" Charlotte huffed. "How can you not? It's so obvious. She doesn't want the police going up and down the elevators? Why?"

"I told you," Lorraine said, "I forgot to call. Can't a person forget? There's so much going on here today."

Charlotte exaggeratedly rolled her eyes. "Likely story."

Clancy, Muriel, and Edna stepped from the crowd and moved toward Skeeter.

"What's going on with all this hurly-burly?" the older man asked.

Skeeter pointed toward the hallway. "We're waiting for Officer Metcalf to return."

"What did you give him them bolt cutters for?"

Charlotte's eyes widened, and Lorraine cocked her head.

"Give it a few minutes," Skeeter said. "Everything will be answered."

From the east hallway, Gayle Goodspeed appeared. Cradled in her arms was Travis. She jerked her head toward the exit.

Skeeter held up his hand and spread his fingers wide.

The marshal mouthed the word 'now' and jerked her head again.

Everyone around Skeeter looked toward Marshal Goodspeed, and her face reddened.

"Who's that woman with your cat?" Clancy asked.

"My grandmother."

A broad smile creased the older man's face. "Well, now. Is that a fact? I think I should go make myself known. See if she needs a tour of this here facility." He held a hand up to his mouth, coughed into it, then smelled the result. Clancy looked toward Skeeter. "Got a breath mint? Never mind. Fortune favors the bold. Wish me luck."

As the older man wandered off, Edna muttered, "Masher."

Muriel clucked. "What a creep. We should make sure our quilt takes twice as long."

"It would serve him right," Edna said.

"Let's make him sort patches first," Muriel said. "Really make him suffer."

The two ladies hurried off to talk with their friends.

Detective Kajal Reddy appeared at the edge of the lobby now. Her forehead glistened as she approached Baggiano. "This better be good. If I have to hoof it back up this building, you're going with me."

The chubby cop nodded. "I understand, Detective, but Skeeter and me—"

Reddy's head snapped toward the assistant maintenance man. "I walked down all those flights for him?"

"Well, we got us a theory—"

The detective interrupted. "You're building theories with Skeeter Dursky? Did someone deputize him and make you two partners? Sort of Skeeter and Hutch?"

"No, ma'am."

Reddy's eyes narrowed. "Then why the heck are you listening to him?"

"He made some good points."

"Good points? This isn't a Hallmark movie, Baggiano. I swear to—"

The detective stopped talking as a hush abruptly descended over the room. Soon whispers of the same word could be heard. "Otto."

Standing at the edge of the lobby was Otto Cantrell. His face was red, as if he had been in the late fall chill for too long. His hair was windswept, his uniform was unkempt, and he only wore one boot. The other foot had a white tube sock on. Next to him was Officer Metcalf— a pair of bolt cutters dangled in his right hand.

Behind them were Carrie Fenton and Shirley Tilson. The two women held hands. Carrie appeared frightened.

Detective Reddy asked Baggiano, "Is that the Fenton woman?"

"I believe so."

"Then arrest her."

Baggiano held up a hand. "Detective, I really think you should wait to hear what Skeeter has to say."

***

Skeeter stood in the middle of the lobby and surveyed all in attendance.

He was over the time limit imposed by Marshal Goodspeed, but the woman seemed to be engaged in a pleasant conversation with Clancy. The older man even jostled some of Travis' fur. The cat swiped a paw at him, and the older man jumped back and rubbed his hand.

When Skeeter's gaze settled on Detective Kajal Reddy, he began. "We've looked at the murder of Mason Freemantle all wrong."

"We?" Detective Reddy asked.

Skeeter didn't want to get on the wrong side of the detective so quickly, but backtracking wouldn't help things either. The best course of action was to press on. "Mason was struck on the head, and his safe was cleared out. The murder weapon was found at the scene as well as forty thousand dollars in a nearby purse."

Murmurs of surprise ran through the crowd. Several people even repeated the amount of money discovered.

"You're telling me things I know," Detective Reddy said. "Get to the point."

"The open safe in Mason's apartment led the responding officers to believe that the money was stolen from there. Cash is hard to trace."

Baggiano emphatically nodded. "Very hard."

Reddy glared at the rotund cop until he stopped bobbing his head.

"The problem," Skeeter continued, "is the killer wasn't after money."

Reddy faced him now. "Wait. This wasn't about the money?"

"No," Skeeter said. He eyed the assistant manager. "Was it, Charlotte?"

Charlotte stepped backward and bumped into the cop with the boot. "How would I know? I had nothing to do with anything."

"Lorraine," Skeeter said, "what is Charlotte's full legal name?"

Sensing an opportunity to redeem herself, Lorraine straightened and pulled her shoulders back. "Her full legal name is Charlotte Ann Thrasher-Olsen. You can check her file in my office."

Skeeter pointed to Officer Baggiano. "And you told me about a plagiarism case that Mason Freemantle defended himself against and won."

The cop nodded, and a smile appeared. "That's right, I did." He glanced around the room and tapped his chest. "I knew that."

Charlotte threw her hands into the air. "What's this got to do with anything?"

"And Officer Baggiano," Skeeter continued, "what happened to that author who brought the case?" He felt like a lawyer cross-examining a witness.

The officer's smile faded. "I don't know what happened to him."

Carrie Fenton raised her hand. "The man killed himself."

A quiet fell over the room.

"That's right," Skeeter said, "the man killed himself." The prosecuting attorneys had repeated witness statements many times during his court cases. For a moment, he wondered if Perry Mason ever did that during the episodes he watched with his grandmother. Skeeter shook the thoughts from his head and pushed forward. "Does anyone know the name of that author?"

The crowd fell silent as they waited for him to provide the answer.

Skeeter lifted a finger, inhaled deeply, and enjoyed the moment of anticipation. "The author was—"

"All right," Charlotte said, "It was my father. So what? It doesn't mean anything."

Most of the residents seemed lost as to what happened. The big reveal that Skeeter was about to give was undercut by Charlotte's flippant revelation. Confused murmurs erupted throughout the crowd.

Skeeter cleared his throat before continuing. "The author who sued Mason Freemantle for plagiarism was Arthur Thrasher—Charlotte's father."

From his place next to Gayle Goodspeed, Clancy hollered, "She already said that, kid.

What's your problem?" He turned to the marshal and said loud enough for the crowd to hear, "You sure he's your grandson?"

The marshal's eyes widened, and she glared at Skeeter.

"You're making me look bad," Baggiano whispered to him. "Wrap it up. These people don't have time to waste."

Skeeter raised his hands for quiet. "What many of you don't know is that Mason Freemantle recently finished his latest manuscript."

"He did!" Shirley Tilson's hands clasped together. "That's right. There was going to be one more City novel. He told us."

The Freemantles whispered excitedly, and Carrie Fenton eyed the older women with open disdain.

"And anyone who is a fan of Mason," Skeeter said, "would know how he wrote his novels. Isn't that right, Shirley?"

Mrs. Tilson waved to her friends on the other side of the lobby. "How Mason wrote his novels? Yes, of course. He wrote them on his typewriter—an IBM Selectric."

"And what did he do with them when he finished?"

Shirley smiled proudly. "He stored them in his safe until his agent picked them up. It's common knowledge. Every fan knows that."

The Freemantles approved her statement by nodding.

"Mason treated his manuscripts like gold,"

Shirley said. "Probably because they were."

Skeeter eyed Charlotte. "Even those who weren't fans could have known about this habit."

The assistant manager frowned. "Why are you looking at me? I don't read the man's work."

Skeeter looked toward Otto and nodded. Metcalf was instructed to tell the older man to remain quiet until it was time. The maintenance supervisor now stepped forward. "That's not true, Charlotte. You've read the man's work."

"How do you know?"

"I saw you throw his books away."

Charlotte shook her head. "Wasn't me."

"Yes," Otto said. "It was. I can prove it."

"How can you prove it?" Skeeter asked.

"I pulled her books from the trash."

Charlotte's eyes widened.

"And why would you do that?" Skeeter asked. "Everyone knows you hate Mason Freemantle."

The maintenance supervisor appeared sheepish. "I did it so I could read them."

"Why would you want to read his books?"

He looked toward Shirley Tilson.

Skeeter smiled. "You did it so you would have something to talk with Mrs. Tilson about."

Shirley seemed genuinely surprised by the revelation. "You did?"

The older man shrugged. "But you were always so focused on Mason, there was never any room for me."

"Oh, Otto. I didn't know."

Detective Reddy leaned over to Skeeter.

"Dang it, Dursky. Stop being a Lifetime movie and get us back on track."

Skeeter cleared his throat. "What is in those books you took from the trash that could prove they were Charlotte's?"

Otto nodded. "She highlighted stuff and wrote in them. The cops should be able to test her handwriting or something."

Charlotte barked a single laugh. "That pseudoscience mumble-jumble won't prove anything. Besides, it was your monkey wrench that killed the man."

"Couldn't have been me." Otto pointed to the heavens. "You locked me up on the roof all afternoon. Thank you for the alibi."

Charlotte said, "You got no proof that I did that."

"Why were you up there?" Skeeter asked.

Otto cast a side-eye glance at Charlotte then turned toward the big man. "Charlotte said Lorraine wanted me to check out the roof. I told her we didn't need another inspection, but she insisted on it. After I got up there, the roof hatch fell down behind me. When I tried to open it, someone had locked it. I've been stuck up there most of the day. I even threw a boot off the side of the building to try and get someone's attention."

A rumble of *ohhhhhs* came from the assembled patrol officers.

The cop with the boot lifted the footwear up. "I think this is yours, Cinderella." He tossed it to Otto.

Skeeter asked, "What happened to your radio?"

Otto pulled on his boot. "Charlotte took it before I went up."

The crowd inhaled reflexively.

"How'd she do that?" Skeeter asked. "How did Charlotte get your radio?"

"She said Lorraine was replacing them."

Charlotte pointed at the manager. "She was. I swear!"

Lorraine shook her head. "I never said that." She turned to the cops. "I never said that."

Clancy stepped forward and put his hands on his hips. "One of them is fibbin'."

"Maybe both," Detective Kajal Reddy added. "Maybe they were in this together."

"I didn't kill Mason Freemantle," Lorraine adamantly said. "I swear."

Skeeter focused on the manager now. "Then what were you doing on the seventeenth floor so quickly after his murder?"

"He invited me up. You were there. You saw."

"You were having a relationship with him." It wasn't a question, and Lorraine blanched at its directness. "But you don't seem broken up by his murder. Why is that?"

Now, the manager looked around.

Charlotte repeatedly pointed at her now. "Because she killed him. That's what I've been trying to say. Can't you see it?"

"No," Skeeter said. "She didn't kill him. She saw the money in the purse, and she thought the same thing all of us did. That Carrie stole some money from Mason Freemantle. Isn't that what you thought?"

Lorraine slowly nodded.

"But you did something that no one thought possible."

The manager blinked repeatedly. "I don't know what you're talking about."

"Neither do I," Detective Reddy said. "What are you holding back, Skeeter?"

"There was more than forty thousand in that purse."

"What!" the detective exclaimed and looked toward Carrie Fenton.

The author looked straight ahead. Her face remained passive as if she were holding a handful of aces at a poker table.

"How do you know that purse had more money, Skeeter?" Detective Reddy asked.

He couldn't say how he knew, so he simply pressed on. "Isn't that right, Lorraine? You stole sixty thousand out of the purse."

The manager adamantly shook her head. "I would never. I didn't have any reason."

"You have past due credit cards," Skeeter said. "Your mortgage is in foreclosure."

Charlotte clapped her hands. "That's true! I saw it in her office. She killed Mason Freemantle."

"No," Lorraine said. "I didn't."

"For part of the afternoon, you've been unavailable to help the police. It wasn't because you didn't want them to solve the murder. It was because you were trying to hide the money."

Detective Reddy put her arm around Lorraine's shoulder. "Here's the thing, Ms. Bagley. If you took some of the money but didn't kill Mason Freemantle that's a non-violent felony. We can work with that."

Lorraine's eyes widened.

"But if you don't tell us where the money is," Reddy said, "I'm going to think you killed the man."

Charlotte clapped again and stomped her foot. "She *did* kill him! Why won't anyone believe me?"

Lorraine glanced around. "I didn't. I promise."

"Then where's the money?"

Tears welled in the manager's eyes. "The bank is threatening to take my house."

"Where's the money?" the crowd cried in unison.

Now, Lorraine sobbed, and her shoulders shook. "It's in the salon."

Skeeter silently chastised himself. It was a place he hadn't searched because it was locked. The business owner wouldn't be back until next week, but he hadn't considered that the building's manager would likely have a key for the suite.

"I found Mason dead," Lorraine continued. "I even yelled for someone to call the police."

Officer Metcalf nodded. "That's what the witnesses told us."

"But when I saw the money in the purse, I sort of lost my mind. I grabbed a bunch of stacks and put them in my pockets. When the cops arrived, I thought for certain someone was going to pat me down."

Reddy eyed Metcalf.

"How was I to know?" the officer said. "I thought she was just lumpy. You know how some people are."

Lorraine continued shaking her head. "The first chance I could leave, I tried to go to my car, but the building was locked down. Then I went to my office, but I realized Charlotte could get in. I couldn't put it in the maintenance room because of you guys." She motioned toward Skeeter then Otto. "That's when I thought of the salon. After putting it away, I came back to you and saw you in my office."

"Why were you so sweaty?"

"I was nervous," she said. "Carrying that much money around with cops in the building tends to do that to a person. I might have taken some of the money, but I could never have killed Mason. I did care for him."

Skeeter turned to Detective Reddy. Slowly, they faced Charlotte.

The assistant manager threw her arms into the air. "You've got to be kidding."

Chapter 21

"You don't have to let us in," Detective Reddy said.

Charlotte waved a hand. "You'll just get a warrant if I don't." The assistant manager unlocked her apartment and pushed the door open. "There you go. Do your worst."

"No," Reddy said. "After you. I insist."

Skeeter and Baggiano followed along.

"Why's he here?" Charlotte pointed to Skeeter.

Detective Reddy eyed the big man. "Stand outside the apartment. This isn't some episode of *Monk*."

Skeeter didn't know what she was talking about, but he moved to the doorway. He rested a shoulder against the jamb and leaned in to hear what was going on.

The detective moved to the bookshelf and removed one of the books. She opened it and inspected it. "Where's the book we took from Otto's room?"

Baggiano pointed to Skeeter, who waggled *The Portland Squeeze*.

Reddy rolled her eyes. "Get in here, Dursky, and show me the handwriting."

Skeeter approached the detective. The two stood side by side and compared the highlighting and notes in each book. The penmanship was the same.

"So what?" Charlotte said. "I threw away some old Mason Freemantle books. It doesn't prove anything."

The detective closed her book. "You lied, though."

"And that's against the law?" Charlotte said. "I didn't want to admit reading that trash."

Skeeter leaned back and looked under the bed. Even though he couldn't see the box, he said, "What's that?"

"What's what?" Reddy asked.

"That box," Skeeter said. "Don't you see it?"

Officer Baggiano had an even worse angle to view underneath the bed than Skeeter. "Yeah. I think I see it. A box, right?"

Detective Reddy knelt and pulled the box from its hiding place. She put it on the bed and opened it. "You could see that from there?"

"Lucky angle," Skeeter said.

"Me too," Baggiano added.

The detective removed the elevator key from the box. "Why's this in here?"

Charlotte appeared aghast. "It wasn't me. I didn't put that there. Someone else must have done it."

Next, the detective lifted the manila folder. She opened it and took a moment to read Arthur Thrasher's obituary. "This confirms the motive for murder."

"No," Charlotte said. "I could never."

"And what's this?" The detective lifted the manuscript. "*The Denver Debacle* by Mason

Freemantle. How did you get this?"

"It was a gift."

"An unpublished manuscript was given to the daughter of the man who sued him for plagiarism?"

Charlotte tried her best to appear innocent. She smiled and looked at everyone in the room. "You didn't know the man. He was a terrible flirt."

"Would he have flirted with you if he knew who you were?" Detective Reddy asked.

Charlotte shrugged. "We'll never know, but I have to assume he would."

"Uh-huh," the detective said. She faced Skeeter. "What I don't understand is the money."

"What about it?" he said. He hadn't come up with an explanation for its existence yet and was hoping something would magically appear to him.

"Where did it come from, and how did it end up in Carrie Fenton's purse?"

Skeeter shrugged. "Where it came from is simple." But it wasn't. He didn't have any divine inspiration. So, he went with the most straightforward thing he could think of. "It was in the safe."

"No, it wasn't," Charlotte blurted.

Everyone turned to stare at her.

The assistant manager's eyes widened, and her face reddened. "I mean, I'm guessing there was no money in the safe."

Baggiano moved to stand next to the

assistant manager.

"Here's the way I figure it," Skeeter said, making it up as he went. "Charlotte planned to kill Mason Freemantle out of revenge for what happened to her father. However, she was waiting for the right time."

Detective Reddy asked, "What made today the right time?"

"Mason finished his latest manuscript. He told Lorraine, Otto, and me that in her office. You can even ask them. When he did so, there was a shadow outside the door. I'm guessing it was Charlotte listening in."

"You've got no proof," the assistant manager said.

Skeeter shrugged. "There was a shadow outside my door later, too. I think Charlotte overheard that conversation as well."

Charlotte rolled her eyes. "Your horoscope dating service. Lame."

Detective Reddy smiled at Skeeter.

The big man shrugged. "A guy must have standards."

"Low ones, apparently," Baggiano muttered.

"Anyway," Skeeter said, "The manuscript is the key. Since Mason stole her father's, she wanted to steal one from him."

"Makes sense to me," Baggiano said.

"Me too," Reddy said.

Skeeter was on a roll and feeling good about his story now. Maybe he'd come up with a plausible tale for Carrie's money after all.

He continued. "Charlotte needed some way to

throw misdirection onto someone else. She lured Otto to the roof and closed the hatch after him. Then she took a heavy tool from the maintenance room—"

"Why didn't she take a hammer?" Detective Reddy asked.

Baggiano nodded. "Or a crowbar? Why not that?"

The three of them looked to Charlotte.

"Why are you looking at me? I don't know anything about anything."

Skeeter shrugged. "Anyway, she caught Mason entering his apartment, and she threatened him with the big wrench." He lifted his hand over his head in a threatening manner. "She told him to open the safe. Mason did what was asked. When she saw all that money, she became momentarily distracted."

"There wasn't any—" Charlotte exclaimed. She quickly covered her mouth. Just as quickly, she uncovered her mouth. "And I didn't kill Mason Freemantle either. I was never there."

Baggiano moved closer to her.

Skeeter mimed a man running. "With her attention diverted, Mason made a break for it, but she hit him over the head. She returned to the safe, and that's when Carrie arrived to finish the argument she had started earlier in the lobby."

Detective Reddy cocked her head. Her brow furrowed as she thought. "So, Charlotte was trapped inside the apartment while Carrie was there. Then Lorraine showed up and started yelling for the cops to be called?"

Skeeter smiled. "That's how I figure it." He was proud of his story and that he was able to make it up on the fly.

"But Lorraine said she saw the money in the purse. How could she—" Reddy motioned toward Charlotte "—put the money into the purse with Lorraine standing there?"

"Right." Skeeter crossed his arms and feigned confusion. "That doesn't make sense."

He had one option now—the truth. "The only answer is Carrie Fenton arrived at Mason Freemantle's apartment with the money inside the purse."

Baggiano chimed in now. "But how can a writer carry around that much money?"

Skeeter didn't have an answer for that, but he fell back on the same response he used when he was a Satan's Dawg. "Is it a crime?"

"We don't know," Detective Reddy said. "Maybe she got it through illegal gains."

The big man shrugged. "You can't go seizing a person's money just because you think it might possibly be illegally gotten. You need probable cause."

It was Detective Reddy's turn to cross her arms. "You sound like an attorney. I think I like you less with each passing minute. Then how did Otto Cantrell's radio get in there?"

Skeeter patted his radio. "Charlotte had planned to leave the murder weapon and Otto's radio there all along. After Lorraine ran away with some of the money, Charlotte simply walked out of the apartment and dropped Otto's radio in the purse."

"Why didn't she take any of the money?" Baggiano asked.

"Because," Detective Reddy said, "this was never about the money."

Charlotte Thrasher-Olsen crossed her arms. "You can't prove any of this."

The detective's eyes narrowed. "We'll see about that. Baggiano, arrest Mrs. Olsen for the murder of Mason Freemantle."

The officer grabbed Charlotte's arm.

Skeeter looked around the apartment. "I bet there's a pair of gloves in here somewhere. Something she might have worn not to get her fingerprints on the radio or the wrench."

"It's Chicago," Charlotte said. "Lots of people wear gloves."

"Already working on your defense," Baggiano muttered.

Detective Reddy headed for the door. "Let's go, Skeeter. Now, I've got to go deal with Carrie Fenton."

***

"Do you want to press charges?"

Carrie Fenton stared at Detective Kajal Reddy. "I'm not sure what you're asking."

"I'm saying do you want us to charge Lorraine Bagley with stealing some of your money?"

Carrie nervously laughed. "No, thank you. Getting it back is enough."

Shirley Tilson stood next to her granddaughter. "I can't believe you have that much money. Why are you carrying it around?"

"Yeah," Reddy asked. "Why *are* you carrying so much cash around?"

Carrie looked to Skeeter, but he simply shrugged.

"I don't trust banks," she said.

The detective's mouth slowly opened then she blew out a large breath of air. "And you thought carrying it around in a leather pouch would be—"

"It's a Bergdorf Goodman," Carrie said. "It cost three thousand."

Detective Reddy's gaze shifted to Skeeter. "Some girl back west, huh?"

The big man shrugged. "I knew she was innocent."

"And you couldn't just tell me?"

"Would you have believed it if I said it?"

"Probably not." She looked toward the elevators. Otto Cantrell was signaling to her. "Looks like my chariot awaits. As soon as we finish our investigation, Carrie, you can have your purse and money back. And you, Skeeter Dursky, don't go too far—just in case I need to ask you some additional questions."

He nodded.

U.S. Marshal Goodspeed sidled up next to Skeeter. She cradled Travis in her arms. The cat seemed quite content with the state of things. "We need to go. They're letting the press in."

Skeeter turned to see the entrance. As he did

so, several members of the press were walking in. Along with them were camera operators who filmed the entire moment. The big man was caught looking directly into a camera. He glanced away, but it was too late. When that made the evening news, it was likely he was going to be made as having been in Chicago.

He looked to Carrie. "I've got to go."

"I know. Thank you for your help. If there's anything I can ever do."

"There is." He eyed Goodspeed before leaning into Carrie's ear. He whispered, "If you ever return to Pleasant Valley—"

The marshal bumped him with her hip. "Let's go, Skeeter."

Carrie met his gaze. "What?"

"Never mind."

He followed Goodspeed toward the exit. Otto hurried up behind them.

"Hey, kid."

Skeeter turned.

"You might have been the shortest-tenured employee I've ever had around here, but I gotta say I liked having you around." The older man stuck out his hand, and Skeeter accepted it. "Take care of yourself and stay outta trouble."

Chapter 22

After putting Travis into the back along with his clothes and book, Beau Smith settled himself into the passenger seat. He turned to observe the tom, who now sat in a small cardboard box with air holes. "Kitty prison. Where'd you get it?"

Marshal Goodspeed didn't respond to his question. Instead, she said, "Buckle up," and waited until he slipped his seatbelt on.

After he did so, he eyed her. "What?"

"Once is chance, twice is a coincidence, and three times is a trend. But what the heck is four? You're making this into a regular habit, and it's getting costly for us."

"It's not my fault."

"The heck it's not. You've blown four covers now." She held up as many fingers. "And what's the common denominator?"

"We've been over this. This wasn't all my fault."

"You say that like it's supposed to make everything better."

"I'm only saying there were more things at play than me."

Goodspeed wagged a finger at him. "Well, Little Sister, you better stop making it a habit because the Marshal Service is running out of ways to hide you."

"Where are we going next?"

"Someplace temporary. Because you blew this up so fast, it's all I've got. It'll have to do. It's a six-week stopgap, but it'll do the trick until I can get you a better fix."

"What is it?"

"It's a place that's going to allow you to wear a disguise. I think I finally figured out a way for you not to stand out."

"Tell me."

"No, but just know that this is my Christmas present to you."

Beau shook his head. "Why did you lie to me about the other witness?"

"Who said I lied?"

"But you said you did."

Marshal Goodspeed chuckled as she turned the ignition key. When the engine fired up, Travis suddenly yowled. It was a loud guttural sound.

"What's wrong with him?" Beau hollered.

"He must not like to travel. A lot of cats are that way. We'll ignore it by turning up the music."

Goodspeed reached for the radio. An annoying disco country song blasted through the radio. The tom wailed louder.

"Only ten hours until we reach our destination," Goodspeed said. "Sit back and relax."

Beau put his head against the window and sighed.

As the car moved through the parking lot,

Officer Baggiano stepped out of the Lake Michigan Tower and waved. Beau was about to wave back when he realized the cop wasn't waving at him. Goodspeed flashed him a thumbs-up as they went by.

"It was him," he said.

"It was who?"

Goodspeed turned up the radio louder. The car left the parking lot of the Lake Michigan Tower, and the marshal abruptly broke into song.

Beau Smith shut his eyes in hopes of blocking out the noise, but it was an impossible task. Instead, he was forced to listen to the radio, the cat, and the marshal as they failed to harmonize about the rhinestone cowboy in a star-spangled rodeo.

Beau Smith
returns in...

**Cozy Up
to Christmas**

ABOUT THE AUTHOR

Colin Conway is the creator of the 509 Crime Stories, a series of novels set in Eastern Washington with revolving lead characters. They are standalone tales and can be read in any order.

He also created the Cozy Up series which pushes the envelope of the cozy genre. Libby Klein, author of the Poppy McAllister series, says *Cozy Up to Death* is "Not your grandma's cozy."

Colin co-authored the Charlie-316 series. The first novel in the series, *Charlie-316*, is a political/crime thriller that has been described as "riveting and compulsively readable," "the real deal," and "the ultimate ride-along."

He served in the U.S. Army and later was an officer of the Spokane Police Department. He's owned a laundromat, invested in a bar, and ran a karate school. Besides writing crime fiction, he is a commercial real estate broker.

Colin lives with his beautiful girlfriend, three wonderful children, and a codependent Vizsla that rules their world.

Learn more at colinconway.com

Made in the USA
Columbia, SC
16 November 2021

49059782R00164